SPECIA ‖‖‖‖‖‖‖ READERS

THE ULVERSCROFT FOUNDATION
(registered UK charity number 264873)

was established in 1972 to provide funds for research, diagnosis and treatment of eye diseases. Examples of major projects funded by the Ulverscroft Foundation are:-

The Children's Eye Unit at Moorfields Eye Hospital, London

The Ulverscroft Children's Eye Unit at Great Ormond Street Hospital for Sick Children

Funding research into eye diseases and treatment at the Department of Ophthalmology, University of Leicester

The Ulverscroft Vision Research Group, Institute of Child Health

Twin operating theatres at the Western Ophthalmic Hospital, London

The Chair of Ophthalmology at the Royal Australian College of Ophthalmologists

You can help further the work of the Foundation by making a donation or leaving a legacy. Every contribution is gratefully received. If you would like to help support the Foundation or require further information, please contact:

THE ULVERSCROFT FOUNDATION
The Green, Bradgate Road, Anstey
Leicester LE7 7FU, England
Tel: (0116) 236 4325

website: www.foundation.ulverscroft.com

P. G. WODEHOUSE

◆

FULL MOON

Complete and Unabridged

ULVERSCROFT
Leicester

First published in Great Britain in 1947 by
Herbert Jenkins
London

This Ulverscroft Edition
published 2018
by arrangement with
Rogers, Coleridge & White Literary Agency
London

A catalogue record for this book is available
from the British Library.

ISBN 978–1–4448–3954–8

1

The refined moon which served Blandings Castle and district was nearly at its full, and the ancestral home of Clarence, ninth Earl of Emsworth, had for some hours now been flooded by its silver rays. They shone on turret and battlement; peeped respectfully in upon Lord Emsworth's sister, Lady Hermione Wedge, as she creamed her face in the Blue Room; and stole through the open window of the Red Room next door, where there was something really worth looking at — Veronica Wedge, to wit, Lady Hermione's outstandingly beautiful daughter, who was lying in bed staring at the ceiling and wishing she had some decent jewellery to wear at the forthcoming County Ball. A lovely girl needs, of course, no jewels but her youth and health and charm, but anybody who had wanted to make Veronica understand that would have had to work like a beaver.

Moving farther afield, the moon picked up Lord Emsworth's brother-in-law, Colonel Egbert Wedge, as he alighted from the station taxi at the front door; and moving still farther, it illuminated Lord Emsworth himself. The ninth earl was down by the pigsty near the kitchen garden, draped in his boneless way over the rail of the bijou residence of Empress of Blandings, his amiable sow, twice in successive years a popular winner in the Fat Pigs class at the Shropshire Agricultural Show.

The ecstasy which always came to the vague and woollen-headed peer when in the society of this noble animal was not quite complete, for she had withdrawn for the night to a sort of covered wigwam in the background and he could not see her. But he could hear her deep, regular breathing, and he was drinking it in as absorbedly as if it had been something from the Queen's Hall conducted by Sir Henry Wood, when the scent of a powerful cigar told him that he was no longer alone. Adjusting his pince-nez, he was astonished to behold the soldierly figure of Colonel Wedge.

The reason he was astonished to behold Colonel Wedge was that he knew the other had gone to London on the previous day to lend his support to the annual banquet of the Loyal Sons of Shropshire. But it was not long before his astute mind had hit upon a possible explanation of his presence in the grounds of Blandings Castle — viz., that he might have come back. And such was indeed the case.

'Ah, Egbert,' he said, courteously uncoiling himself.

Going for a stroll to stretch his legs after his long journey, Colonel Wedge had supposed himself to be alone with Nature. The shock of discovering that what he had taken for a pile of old clothes was alive and a relation by marriage caused him to speak a little sharply.

'Good God, Clarence, is that you? What on

earth are you doing out here at this time of night?'

Lord Emsworth had no secrets from his nearest and dearest. He replied that he was listening to his pig, and the statement caused his companion to wince as if some old wound had troubled him. Egbert Wedge had long held the view that the head of the family into which he had married approached more closely to the purely cuckoo every time he saw him, but this seemed to mark a bigger stride in that direction than usual.

'Listening to your pig?' he said, in an almost awe-struck voice, and paused for a moment, digesting this information. 'You'd better come in and go to bed. You'll be getting lumbago again.'

'Perhaps you are right,' agreed Lord Emsworth, and fell into step at the other's side.

For a while they proceeded towards the house in a restful silence, each busy with his own thoughts. Then, as so often happens on these occasions, both spoke simultaneously, the colonel saying that he had run into Freddie last night and Lord Emsworth asking if his companion, when in London, had gone to see Mabel.

This puzzled the colonel.

'Mabel?'

'I mean Dora. I forgot her name for the moment. My sister Dora.'

'Oh, Dora? Good God, no. When I go to London for a day's pleasure, I don't waste my time seeing Dora.'

The sentiment was one of which Lord

Emsworth thoroughly approved. It made him feel that his brother-in-law was a man of taste and discernment.

'Of course not, my dear fellow, naturally not,' he hastened to say. 'Nobody in their senses would. Silly of me to have asked. I wrote to Dora the other day, asking her to find me an artist to paint the portrait of my pig, and she wrote back most rudely, telling me not to be ridiculous. Bless my soul, what a horrible collection of pests the female members of my family are. Dora is bad enough, but look at Constance, look at Julia. Above all, look at Hermione.'

'My wife,' said Colonel Wedge stiffly.

'Yes,' said Lord Emsworth, giving his arm a sympathetic little pat. 'Now why,' he mused, 'did I ask you if you had seen Dora? There was some reason. Ah, yes, Hermione had a letter from her this morning. Dora is very worried.'

'Why?'

'Oh, extremely worried.'

'What about?'

'I haven't a notion.'

'Didn't Hermione tell you?'

'Oh, she *told* me,' said Lord Emsworth, with the air of one conceding a minor point. 'She explained the circumstances fully. But what they were I have completely forgotten. Except that it was something to do with rabbits.'

'Rabbits?'

'So Hermione said.'

'Why the deuce should Dora be worried about rabbits?'

'Ah,' said Lord Emsworth, as if feeling that he

was being taken into deep waters. Then, brightening: 'Perhaps they have been eating her lobelias.'

A sharp snort escaped Colonel Wedge.

'Your sister Dora,' he said, 'lives on the fourth floor of Wiltshire House, Grosvenor Square, a block of residential flats in the heart of London. So she has no lobelias.'

'Then it is difficult to see,' agreed Lord Emsworth, 'how rabbits can have entered into the thing. Tell me,' he proceeded, shelving a topic which had never really gripped his interest, 'did I hear you say that you had had a letter from Freddie?'

'I said I had met him.'

'Met him?'

'In Piccadilly. He was with a tight chap.'

'A tight chap?'

Colonel Wedge's temper was inclined to be short, and a *tête-à-tête* with the rambling old backwoodsman at his side never improved it. The latter's habit of behaving like a Swiss mountain echo or the member of the cross-talk team who asks the questions might well have irritated a more patient man.

'Yes, a tight chap. A young man under the influence of alcoholic liquor. You know what a tight chap is.'

'Oh, quite, quite. A tight chap, yes, certainly. But it couldn't have been Freddie, my dear fellow. No, not Freddie. Somebody else, perhaps.'

Colonel Wedge clenched his teeth. A weaker man might have gnashed them.

5

'It was Freddie, I tell you. Do you think I don't know Freddie when I see him? Why the devil shouldn't it have been Freddie?'

'He's in America.'

'He is not in America.'

'He is,' persisted Lord Emsworth stoutly. 'Don't you remember? He married the daughter of an American dog-biscuit manufacturer and went to live in America.'

'He's been back in England for weeks.'

'Bless my soul!'

'His father-in-law sent him over to whack up the English end of the concern.'

Once again Lord Emsworth blessed his soul. He found the idea of his younger son, the Hon. Freddie Threepwood, whacking up English ends of concerns almost incredible. Years of association with the boy had left him with the opinion that he had just about enough intelligence to open his mouth when he wanted to eat, but certainly no more.

'His wife came with him, but she has gone on to Paris. Freddie's coming down here to-morrow.'

Lord Emsworth gave a quick, convulsive leap, then became strangely rigid. Like so many fathers of the English upper classes, he was somewhat allergic to younger sons, and was never at his happiest when entertaining the one whom an unkind Fate had added to his quiver. Freddie, when at Blandings, had a way of mooning about looking like a bored and despairing sheep, with glassy eyes staring out over an eleven-inch cigarette holder, which had always been enough to bring a black frost into this Eden of his.

'Coming here? Freddie?' A numbness seemed to be paining his sense, as though of hemlock he had drunk. 'He won't be staying long, will he?' he asked, with a father's pathetic eagerness.

'Weeks and weeks and weeks, I gathered. If not months. In fact, he spoke as if he intended to stay indefinitely. Oh, and I forgot to mention it, he's bringing the tight chap with him. Good night, Clarence, good night,' said Colonel Wedge buoyantly. And, his cheerfulness completely restored by the reflection that he had ruined his relative's beauty sleep, he proceeded to the Blue Room to report to his wife, who had finished creaming her face and was now in bed, skimming the pages of a novel.

II

She glanced up as he entered with a pleased cry.

'Egbert!'

'Hullo, my dear.'

Unlike the rest of the female members of her family, who were tall and stately, Lady Hermione Wedge was short and dumpy and looked like a cook — in her softer moods, a cook well satisfied with her latest soufflé; when stirred to anger, a cook about to give notice; but always a cook of strong character. Nevertheless, for the eye of love is not affected by externals, it was with courtly devotion that her husband, avoiding the face cream, bent and kissed the top of her boudoir

7

cap. They were a happy and united couple. Most of those who came into contact with this formidable woman shared Lord Emsworth's opinion of her, trembling — like Ben Bolt's Alice — with fear at her frown, but Colonel Wedge had never for an instant regretted having said: 'Eh? Oh, rather, yes, certainly,' in reply to the clergyman's: 'Wilt thou, Egbert, take this Hermione — ?' Where others quailed before her commanding eye, he merely admired it.

'Well, here I am at last, old girl,' he said. 'The train was a bit late, and I've just been for a stroll in the garden. I ran into Clarence.'

'He wasn't out in the garden?'

'Yes, he was. Courting lumbago, and so I told him. What's all this Dora business? I met young Prudence this morning as I was passing through Grosvenor Square — she was airing those dogs of hers — but she never said a word about it. Clarence says you told him she was being worried by rabbits.'

Lady Hermione tut-tutted, as she had so often been compelled to tut-tut when her brother was the subject of the conversation.

'I wish Clarence would occasionally listen to one, instead of just gaping with his mouth open and not paying the slightest attention to what one is saying. What I told him was that Dora was worried because a man has been calling Prudence a dream rabbit.'

'Oh, was that it? Who was the man?'

'She hasn't the remotest idea. That is why she is so worried. It seems that yesterday her butler came and asked where Prudence was, as a

8

gentleman wished to speak to her on the telephone. Prudence was out, so Dora went to the telephone, and a strange male voice said: 'Hullo, my precious dream rabbit.''

'And what did she do?'

'Bungled everything, as you would expect her to do. Dora really has no sense whatever. Instead of waiting to hear more, she said that this was Prudence's mother speaking. Upon which the man gave a sort of gasp and rang off. Of course she questioned Prudence when she came in, and asked her who it was that called her a dream rabbit, and Prudence said it might have been anyone.'

'Something in that. Everyone seems to call everyone everything nowadays.'

'Not 'dream rabbit'.'

'You would consider that pretty strong stuff?'

'I know I should make the most searching enquiries about any young man whom I heard calling Veronica a dream rabbit. I don't wonder Dora is uneasy. She tells me Prudence has been seeing a great deal of Galahad recently, and goodness knows whom he may not have introduced to her. Galahad's idea of a suitable friend for an impressionable young girl might quite easily be a race-course tout or a three-card-trick man.'

Colonel Wedge was exhibiting that slight sheepishness which comes to married men when the names of those whom they themselves esteem highly but of whom they are aware that their wives disapprove crop up in the course of conversation. He knew that his affection and

9

admiration for Lord Emsworth's younger brother, the Hon. Galahad Threepwood, was not shared by the latter's sisters, who considered that *beau sabreur* and man about town a blot on the escutcheon of a proud family.

'Some of Gally's pals are queer fish,' he admitted. 'One of them once picked my pocket. He was at the dinner.'

'The pickpocket?'

'No, Gally.'

'He would be.'

'Oh, come, old girl, don't speak as if it had been an orgy. And whatever sort of a life Gally has led, by George it's agreed with him. I never saw a man looking fitter. He's coming here for Vee's birthday.'

'I know,' said Lady Hermione, without pleasure. 'And Freddie. Did Clarence tell you that Freddie would be here to-morrow with a friend?'

'Eh? No, I told him. I happened to run into Freddie in Piccadilly. You don't mean Clarence knew all the time? Well, I'm dashed. When I mentioned to him just now that Freddie was headed for the castle, the news came as a complete surprise and bowled him over.'

'His vagueness is really very trying.'

'Vagueness?' Colonel Wedge came of a long line of bluff military men who called spades spades. He would have none of these polite euphemisms. 'It isn't vagueness. It's sheer, gibbering lunacy. The fact is, old girl, we've got to face it, Clarence is dotty. He was dotty when I

10

married you, twenty-four years ago, and he's been getting dottier and dottier ever since. Where do you think I found him just now? Down at the pigsty. I noticed something hanging over the rail, and thought the pig man must have left his overalls there, and then it suddenly reared itself up like a cobra and said 'Ah, Egbert.' Gave me a nasty shock. I nearly swallowed my cigar. Questioned as to what the deuce he thought he was playing at, he said he was listening to his pig.'

'Listening to his pig?'

'I assure you. And what, you will ask, was the pig doing? Singing? Reciting 'Dangerous Dan McGrew'? Nothing of the kind. Just breathing. I tell you, the idea of being cooped up at Blandings Castle at the time of the full moon with Clarence, Galahad, Freddie, and this fellow Plimsoll on the premises is one that frankly appals me. It'll be like being wrecked on a desert island with the Marx Brothers.'

'Plimsoll?'

'This chap Freddie's bringing down.'

'Is his name Plimsoll?'

'Well, I've only Freddie's word for it, of course. The chap himself was too blotto to utter. During our conversation he stood silently supporting himself with one hand against a cab shelter and catching invisible flies with the other, a sort of sweet, fixed smile on his face. I never saw a fellow so completely submerged.'

A wrinkle had come into Lady Hermione's forehead, as if she were trying to stimulate her memory.

'What was he like?'

'Tall, thin chap. About Clarence's build. In fact, if you can picture a young, intoxicated Clarence with a beaky nose and horn-rimmed spectacles, you will have a very fair idea of Plimsoll. Why, do you know him?'

'I'm trying to remember. I have certainly heard the name before. Did Freddie tell you anything about him?'

'He hadn't time. You know how it is when you meet Freddie. Your impulse is to hurry on. I just paused long enough for him to mention that he was coming to Blandings with this fly-catching chap and that the fly-catching chap's name was Tipton Plimsoll, and then I sprang into a cab.'

'Tipton! Of course! Now I remember.'

'You do know him?'

'We have never met, but he was pointed out to me in a restaurant just before we left London. He is a young American, educated in England, I believe, and very rich.'

'Rich?'

'Enormously rich.'

'Good God!'

There was a pause. They looked at each other. Then, as if by mutual consent, their eyes strayed to the wall on the left, behind which Veronica Wedge lay gazing at the ceiling. Lady Hermione's breathing had become more rapid, and on the colonel's face, as he sat silently playing This Little Pig Went to Market with his consort's toes, there was the look of one who sees visions.

He coughed.

'He will be nice company for Vee.'

'Yes.'

'Do her all the good in the world.'

'Yes.'

'It's — er — an excellent thing for young people — in a place like this — depths of the country and all that — to have young people to talk to. Brightens them up.'

'Yes. Did he seem nice?'

'A charming personality, I thought. Allowing, of course, for the fact that he was as soused as a herring.'

'I don't attach much importance to that. He probably has not a very strong head.'

'No. And a fellow spending the evening with Freddie would naturally have to keep himself going. Besides, there is always this to bear in mind — Vee isn't hard to please.'

'What do you mean?'

'Well, dash it, when you reflect that she was once engaged to Freddie — '

'Oh dear, I had forgotten that. I must tell her not to mention it. And you had better warn Clarence.'

'I'll go and see him now. Good night, old girl.'

'Good night, dear.'

There was a rather rapt look on Colonel Wedge's clean-cut face as he left the room. He was not a man given to any great extent to the dreaming of daydreams, but he had fallen into one now. He seemed to be standing in the library of Blandings Castle, his hand on the shoulder of a tall, thin young man in horn-rimmed spectacles who had asked if he could have a word with him in private.

'Pay your addresses to my daughter, Plimsoll?' he was saying. '*Certainly* you may pay your addresses to my daughter, my dear fellow.'

III

In the Red Room Veronica was still thinking about the County Ball, and not too optimistically. She would have liked to be in a position to attend that function glittering like a chandelier, but of this she felt there was little hope. For though she would be twenty-three years old in a few days, experience had taught her not to expect diamond necklaces on her birthday. The best the future seemed to hold was the brooch promised her by her uncle Galahad and an unspecified trinket at which her cousin Freddie had hinted.

Her reverie was interrupted by the opening of the door. The pencil of light beneath it had attracted Colonel Wedge's eye as he started forth on his mission. She raised her head from the pillow and rolled two enormous eyes in his direction. In a slow, pleasant voice, like clotted cream made audible, she said:

'Hullo, Dad-dee.'

'Hullo, my dear. How are you?'

'All right, Dad-dee.'

Colonel Wedge seated himself on the end of the bed, amazed afresh, as he always was when he saw this daughter of his, that two such parents as his wife and himself, mere selling platers in the way of looks, could have produced an offspring so spectacular. Veronica Wedge, if the dumbest, was certainly the most beautiful girl registered among the collateral branches in the pages of Debrett's Peerage. With the brains of a peahen, and one whose mental growth had been retarded by being dropped on its head when just out of the egg, she combined a radiant loveliness which made fashionable photographers fight for her custom. Every time you saw in the paper the headlines

WEST END AFFRAY
PHOTOGRAPHERS BRAWL WHILE
THOUSANDS CHEER

you could be pretty certain that trade rivalry concerning Veronica Wedge had caused the rift.

'When did you get back, Dad-dee?'

'Just now. Train was late.'

'Did you have a nice time in London?'

'Very nice. Quite a good dinner. Your uncle Galahad was there.'

'Uncle Gally's coming here for my birthday.'

'So he told me. And Freddie arrives to-morrow.'

'Yes.'

Veronica Wedge spoke without emotion. If the severing of her engagement to Frederick Threepwood and his union with another had ever pained her, it was clear that the agony had abated.

'He's bringing a friend with him. Chap named Tipton Plimsoll.'

'Oh, is that who it is?'

15

'You've met him?'

'No, but I was at Quaglino's with Mummie one day, and somebody pointed him out. He's frightfully rich. Does Mummie want me to marry him?'

There was an engaging simplicity and directness about his child which sometimes took Colonel Wedge's breath away. It did so now.

'Good God!' he said, when he had recovered it. 'What an extraordinary notion. I don't suppose such an idea so much as crossed her mind.'

Veronica lay thinking for a few moments. It was a thing she did very seldom and then only with the greatest difficulty, but this was a special occasion.

'I wouldn't mind,' she said. 'He didn't look a bad sort.'

Her words were not burning — Juliet, speaking of Romeo, would have put it better — but they came as music to Colonel Wedge. It was with uplifted heart that he kissed his daughter good night. He had reached the door, when it occurred to him that there was a subject he had intended to touch on the next time he saw her.

'Oh, by the way, Vee, has anyone ever called you a dream rabbit?'

'No, Dad-dee.'

'Would you consider it pretty significant if they did? Even nowadays, I mean, when everybody calls everyone every dashed thing under the sun — 'darling' and 'angel' and all that sort of thing?'

'Oh yes, Dad-dee.'

itself upon an observer on the present occasion was the fact that she appeared extraordinarily happy. She had, indeed, the air of a girl who is thoroughly above herself. Her eyes were shining, her feet seemed to dance along the pavement, and from her lips there proceeded a gay song, not so loudly as to disturb the amenities of Grosvenor Square, but loudly enough to shock a monocled young man who had just come up behind her, causing him to prod her in the small of the back with an austere umbrella.

'Less of it, young Prue,' he said rebukingly. 'You can't do that there here.'

The clocks, as has been stated, showed that the time was only twenty minutes past nine. Nevertheless, this musical critic was Lord Emsworth's younger son, Freddie. Early though the hour was, Frederick Threepwood was up and about, giving selfless service to the firm which employed him. Sent over to London to whack up the English end of Donaldson's Inc., manufacturers of the world-famous Donaldson's Dog-Joy, he had come to catch his aunt Dora before she went out and give her a sales talk.

The thing was, of course, a mere incident in a busy man's routine. Lady Dora Garland was not, like some women, a sort of projecting rock in the midst of a foaming sea of dogs, and flags would not be run up over the firm's Long Island City factory if he booked her order; but as the managing director of two distinct spaniel and an Irish setter she was entitled to her place as a prospect. Allowing, say, twenty biscuits per day per spaniel and the same or possibly more per

21

day per Irish setter, her custom per year per complete menagerie would be quite well worth securing. Your real go-getter, seething though his brain may be with gigantic schemes, does not disdain these minor coups, for he knows that every little bit added to what you've got makes just a little bit more.

The apparition of her cousin seemed to astonish Prudence as much as that of Colonel Wedge on the previous night had astonished Lord Emsworth.

'Golly, Freddie,' she cried, amazed. 'Up already?'

The poetic greeting plainly stung the young go-getter.

'Already? What do you mean, already? Why, over in Long Island City I leave the hay at seven sharp, and by nine-thirty we're generally half-way through our second conference.'

'You don't attend conferences?'

'You betcher I attend conferences.'

'Well, you could knock me down with a feather,' said Prudence composedly. 'I always thought you were a sort of office boy.'

'Me? Vice-president. Say, is Aunt Dora in?'

'She was just going to the phone when I came out. Somebody ringing up from Blandings.'

'Good. I want a talk with her. I've been trying to get around to it for days. It's about those dogs of yours. What do they live on?'

'The chairs most of the time.'

Freddie clicked his tongue. One smiles at these verbal pleasantries, but they clog the wheels of commerce.

'I am not referring to the university of that name, but to a pub on the outskirts called the Mulberry Tree. I used to frequent it a good deal, and every time I went this bird was there. The story was that he was being paid to haunt the place.'

'It belonged to his uncle.'

'Did it? Then that explains why he was so glued to the premises. Well, what with him constantly being there and me constantly popping in for lunch, dinner, or possibly only a drink, we became close cronies. Lister was his name.'

'It still is.'

'Bill Lister. We used to call him Blister. And he was, as you say, an artist. I remember thinking it rummy. Somehow the life artistic didn't seem to go with a face like that.'

'What do you mean, a face like that?'

'Well, it is, isn't it?'

'Your own dial, young Freddie,' said Prudence coldly, 'is nothing to write home about. I think Bill's lovely. How odd that you should be friends.'

'Not at all. Blister was loved by all who knew him.'

'I mean, how odd that you should have known him.'

'Not in the least. You couldn't look in at the Mulberry Tree without bumping into him. He seemed to fill up all the available space. And having bumped into him, one naturally fraternized. So his uncle owns that joint, does he?'

'Not now. He died the other day, and left it to Bill.'

'Any dogs there?'

'How on earth should I know?'

A keen look had come into Freddie's eyes.

'Ask Blister. And, if there are, put him in touch with me. Well,' said Freddie, returning to his breast pocket the notebook in which he had made a swift entry, 'this sounds like a bit of bunce for my old friend. Taking into consideration goodwill, fixtures, stock in cellar, and so forth, he should be able to sell out for a fairish sum.'

'But that's just the point. I don't want him to sell out. I want him to chuck being an artist and run the Mulberry Tree. It's the most wonderful opportunity. He'll never get anywhere, muddling along with his painting, and we could make a fortune out of a place like that. It's just the right distance from Oxford, which gives us a ready-made clientele, and we could put in a squash court and a swimming pool and advertise it in the London papers, and it might become as popular as that place in Buckinghamshire that everybody goes to. Of course, we should need capital.'

Except when exercised in the interests of the dog biscuits so ably manufactured by the father of his charming wife, Freddie Threepwood's was not a particularly alert mind, but a duller man than he, listening to this speech, would have been able to detect an oddness in his companion's choice of pronouns.

'We?'

'Bill and I are going to be married.'

'Well, I'm blowed. You love this Blister?'

'Madly.'

'And he loves you?'

'Frightfully.'

'Well, I'm dashed. What does Aunt Dora think about it?'

'She hasn't heard about it yet.'

Freddie was looking grave. He was fond of this young peanut, and he feared for her happiness.

'I doubt if she's going to clap her little hands much.'

'No.'

'I wouldn't say a word against Aunt Dora, so I won't call her England's leading snob.'

'Mother's a darling.'

'A darling, maybe, though I confess I've never seen that side of her. But you can't say she isn't a bit acutely alive to the existence of class distinctions. And what I feel is that when you inform her that *il promessi sposi* had an uncle who ran a pub . . . But perhaps this uncle was just an unfortunate accident such as happens in the hottest families. Blister's father, you are possibly about to tell me, was of the noblesse?'

'He was a sporting journalist. Uncle Gally met him in a pub.'

'Pubs do seem to enter into this romance of yours, don't they? His mother?'

'A Strong Woman on the music-hall stage. One of Uncle Gally's dearest friends. She's been dead for a good many years, but he tells me that when she was in her prime she could take the poker and tie it into a lover's knot with one hand.'

'That's where Blister gets his physique?'

'I suppose so.'

Freddie removed his monocle and polished it. His face was graver than ever.

'Totting up the score, then, the best we can credit Blister with is a kind heart and a pub.'

'Yes.'

'For you, of course, that is enough. Kind hearts, you say to yourself, are more than coronets. But what of Aunt Dora? I have a feeling that the fact that Blister is Uncle Gally's godson won't carry much weight. I doubt if you can count on her blessing as an absolute snip.'

'The very thought that crossed my mind,' said Prudence. 'That's why we are having a quiet wedding this morning at the Brompton Road Registry Office without telling her.'

'What!'

'Yes.'

'Well, strike me pink!'

'I've got the whole thing worked out. What I feel is that we must confront the family with a . . . What's that French expression?'

'Oo la la?'

'Fait accompli. What I feel we need here is a fait accompli. When you confront people with fait accompli's you've got 'em cold. You see, as I was saying, in order to develop this pub of Bill's as it should be developed, we shall need quite a bit of capital. That will have to come from Uncle Clarence.'

'You consider him the people's choice?'

'Well, he's the head of the family. A head of a family can't let his niece down. He's practically got to rally round her. So what I feel is, dish out the *fait accompli*, and then go to Uncle Clarence and say: 'Here's this wonderful business opportunity, needing only a mere fraction of your heaped-up wealth to turn it into a bonanza. I'm your niece. Bill's just become your nephew. Blood is thicker than water. So how about it?' It seems to me that we're doing the only sane, prudent thing in getting married at the Brompton Road Registry Office.'

Her girlish enthusiasm had begun to infect Freddie. His, too, he could not but remember, had been a runaway match, and look what a ball of fire that had turned out. As he thought of the day when he and Niagara ('Aggie') Donaldson had skimmed around the corner and become man and wife, a wave of not unmanly sentiment poured over him.

'I guess you're about right, at that.'

'Oh, Freddie, you're a darling.' Prudence's blue eyes glowed with affection and gratitude for this cousinly support. She told herself that she had always been devoted to this prince of dog-biscuit pedlars, and a spasm of remorse shook her as she recalled that at the age of ten she had once knocked off his top hat with a well-directed half brick. 'Your sympathy and moral support mean so much to us. Are you doing anything this morning?'

'Nothing special. I want to have this conference with Aunt Dora, and then I've got to look in at Aspinall's in Bond Street. Apart from that I'm fairly free.'

'What are you doing at Aspinall's? Buying a birthday present for Vee?'

'I thought of getting her a pendant there. But what I'm really looking in about is Aggie's necklace. A rather unfortunate situation has arisen. She left the damn thing with me to take to Aspinall's to be cleaned, and what with one thing and another it's kept slipping my mind. She needs it, it seems, for the various routs and revels into which she has been plunged since her arrival in the gay city, and she's been wiring about it a good deal. The communication which reached me this morning was rather a stinker, and left me with the impression that further delay might be fatal. Why did you ask if I was doing anything this morning? Do you want me to roll up?'

'If you would. Bill's sure to forget to bring a witness. He's rather got the jumps, poor angel. And I don't want to have the driver of the taxi.'

'I know what you mean. When Aggie and I were put through it, we had to fall back on the charioteer, and he spoiled the party. A bit too broadly jocular for my taste, besides wanting to muscle in on the wedding breakfast. But won't Uncle Gally be on the spot? He seems to have been more or less the sponsor of this binge.'

'You don't expect Uncle Gally to be up by twelve, do you? He probably didn't get to bed till six or seven, poor lamb. No, it must be you. Do come, Freddie, my beautiful Freddie.'

'I'll be there. We Threepwoods stand by our

32

pals. I shall have to bring a guy named Plimsoll.'

'Oh, why?'

'Imperative. I'm taking him down to Blandings later in the day, and I daren't let him out of my sight during the luncheon hour or he might vanish on a jag. I've got a colossal deal pending with the man.'

'Is he somebody special?'

'You bet he's somebody special. He's Tipton's.'

'What's that?'

'Haven't you ever heard of Tipton's? Shows you've not been in America. Tipton's Stores have branches in every small town throughout the Middle West. They supply the local yokels with everything, including dog biscuits. I should estimate that the dog biscuits sold annually by Tipton's, if placed end to end, would reach from the rock-bound coast of Maine to the Everglades of Florida. Possibly further.'

'And Plimsoll is really Tipton in disguise? When I meet him and say: 'Hullo there, Plimsoll,' will he tear off his whiskers and shout: 'April Fool! I'm Tipton'?'

Freddie was obliged to click his tongue once more.

'Plimsoll owns the controlling interest in Tipton's,' he explained austerely. 'And my aim is to talk him into giving Donaldson's Inc. the exclusive dog-biscuit concession throughout his vast system of chain stores. If I can swing it, it will be about the biggest thing we've ever pulled off.'

'Your father-in-law will be pretty bucked.'

'He'll go capering about Long Island City like a nautch girl.'

'I should think he would make you . . . Is there anything higher than a vice-president?'

'Well, as a matter of fact,' Freddie confessed, in a burst of candour, 'in most of these American concerns, as far as I've been able to make out, vice-president is about where you start. I fancy my guerdon ought to be something more on the lines of assistant sales manager.'

'Well, good luck, anyway. How do the prospects look?'

'Sometimes bright. Sometimes not so bright. You see, old Tippy only got control of his money a couple of months ago, and he has been celebrating almost without a break ever since.'

'He sounds the sort of man Uncle Gally would like. Twin souls.'

'And the difficulty I have had to contend with has been to catch him at the psychological moment for getting him to sign on the dotted line. He's either been too plastered to hold a pen, or else in the grip of the sort of hangover which makes a man lose interest in everything except bicarb of soda. That's why it's such a terrific strategic move having got him to let me take him to Blandings. He won't find the same facilities there as in London.'

'And he won't be able to get away, when you corner him and start yelling about the broad Donaldson highroad.'

'Exactly. I had omitted to take that into my calculations. Well, I mustn't stand talking to you all the morning, young dogface. Where did you say the fixture was?'

'Brompton Road Registry Office. It's just beyond the Park Hotel.'

'And the kick-off is timed for — ?'

'Twelve sharp.'

'Fine. That will give me nice time to sow the good seed with Aunt Dora and go to the jewel bin. Then a quick phone call to Tippy, telling him where and when to meet me, and I'll be with you.'

'Don't go dropping any incautious words to Mother.'

'My dear child! You know me. On the subject of your romance I shall of course seal my lips completely. And when I seal my lips,' said Freddie, 'they stay sealed.'

★   ★   ★

It was some twenty minutes later that he came out of Wiltshire House. When he did so, his face was grave and perplexed. The process of sowing the good seed with his aunt Dora had been attended by none of the success to which he had looked forward with such bright anticipation. True to his promise, he had sealed his lips regarding the forthcoming proceedings at the Brompton Road Registry Office, and it seemed to him that he might just as well have sealed them on the subject of dog biscuits.

To say that he had actually been given the sleeve across the windpipe by his relative would perhaps be too much. But he had found her in strange mood, her manner distrait and preoccupied and with more than a suggestion in it of wishing to be alone. The best he had been able to achieve had been an undertaking on her part that, if sent a free sample, she would give it a trial; and, as he returned to his headquarters after fulfilling his wife's commission and giving orders for Veronica's birthday present, he was realizing how those charmers must have felt who suffered from the sales resistance of the deaf adder.

Arrived at his rooms, he established telephonic communication with that haunt of the gilded rich, Barribault's Hotel in Brook Street, and asked to be connected with Mr Plimsoll. And presently a rather hoarse and roopy voice came to him over the wire, the voice of one who at no distant date has been wandering long and far across the hot sands.

'Hello?'

'What ho, Tippy. This is Freddie.'

'Oh, hello, Freddie. You caught me just in time. Another second, and I'd have been gone.'

'Where are you off to?'

'Going to see a doctor.'

Freddie cooed sympathetically.

'Feeling bad?'

'No, as a matter of fact I'm feeling extraordinarily well. Most amazingly well. You would be astounded if you knew how well I'm feeling. But a number of light pink spots appear to have sprouted on my chest. Have you ever had pink spots on your chest?'

'I don't think so.'

'It isn't a question of thinking. You've either got 'em or you haven't. There is no middle course. Mine are a curious rosy colour, like the first flush of the sky on a summer morning. I thought it might be as well to have the medicine man cock an eye at them. I never had measles as a child.'

'Why not?'

'Ah, that's what we would all like to know. I dare say, if the truth came out, it would rock civilization.'

'Well, can you meet me at twelve at the Brompton Road Registry Office? A pal of mine is getting married there.'

'Now, there's a sap's game, if you like. However, I hope he'll be happy. I don't say he will, mind you. It's just a kindly hope. Okay. Brompton Road Registry Office, twelve o'clock.'

'It's near the Park Hotel. I'll give you lunch there.'

'Excellent.'

'I'll come in the car, so bring your things. Then we can start straight off for Blandings afterwards.'

'Blandings?'

'I'd like to get there for dinner.'

'Blandings,' said Mr Plimsoll. 'Of course, yes, Blandings. I knew there was something I wanted to tell you. I'm not coming to Blandings.'

It was not easy to make Freddie Threepwood shake like an aspen. Usually, in order to shatter his iron composure, you had to praise Peterson's Pup Food in his hearing. But he shook now perceptibly and just like an aspen.

'What!'

'No. Where's the sense in burying myself in the country when I'm feeling so extraordinarily well? The whole point of the scheme, if you remember, was that I should go there and tone up my system by breathing pure air. But now that it's gone and toned itself up, I don't need pure air. In fact, I'd rather not have it.'

'But, Tippy . . . '

'It's off,' said Mr Plimsoll firmly. 'We wash the project out. This other idea of yours, however, of standing me a bite of lunch, strikes me as admirable. I'll come dashing up, all fire and ginger. You'll know me by the rosy cheeks. I really am feeling astoundingly well. It's what I've always said — alcohol's a tonic. Where most fellows go wrong is that they don't take enough of it. Twelve o'clock at the what's-its-name. Good. Right. Fine. Swell. Capital. Excellent. Splendid,' said Mr Plimsoll, and rang off.

For some moments Freddie stood motionless. This shattering blow to his hopes and dreams had temporarily stunned him. He toyed with the idea of calling the other back and reasoning with him. Then he reflected that this could be better done quietly and at one's leisure across the luncheon table. He lit a cigarette, and there came into his face a look of stern determination. Donaldson's Inc. trains its vice-presidents well. They may be down, but they are never out.

As for Mr Plimsoll, he picked up hat and umbrella, balanced the latter buoyantly on his chin for an instant, then went out and rang for the elevator. A few minutes later he was being assisted into a taxi by the ex-King of Ruritania who patrolled the sidewalk in front of the main entrance.

'Harley Street,' he said to the driver. 'And don't spare the horses.'

Harley Street, as everybody knows, is where medical men collect in gangs, and almost every door you see has burst out into a sort of eczema of brass plates. At a house about half-way down the thoroughfare the following members of the healing profession had elected to mess in together: Hartley Rampling, P. P. Borstal, G. V. Cheesewright, Sir Abercrombie Fitch-Fitch, and E. Jimpson Murgatroyd. The one Tipton was after was E. Jimpson Murgatroyd.

3

The great drawback to choosing a doctor at random out of the telephone directory just because you like his middle name — Tipton had once been engaged to a girl called Doris Jimpson — is that until you are in his consulting room and it is too late to back out, you don't know what you are going to get. It may be a kindred soul, or it may be someone utterly alien and unsympathetic. You are taking a leap in the dark.

The moment Tipton set eyes on E. Jimpson Murgatroyd he knew that he had picked a lemon in the garden of medicine. What he had hoped for was a sunny practitioner who would prod him in the ribs with his stethoscope, compliment him on his amazing health, tell him an anecdote about a couple of Irishmen named Pat and Mike, give him some sort of ointment for the spots, and send him away in a whirl of good-fellowship. And E. Jimpson proved to be a gloomy man with side whiskers, who smelled of iodoform and had obviously been looking on the black side of things since he was a slip of a boy.

Seeming not in the least impressed by Tipton's extraordinary fitness, he had asked him in a low, despondent voice to take a seat and show him his spots. And when he had seen them he shook his head and said he didn't like those spots. Tipton

which had animated him in the lobby of Barribault's. Once more the mere quivering jelly of nerves he had been since he had woken to the realization that this was his wedding day, he panted for these quick ones as the hart pants for cooling streams when heated in the chase.

And it was as he drew abreast of the Park Hotel, which stands but a stone's throw from the Brompton Road Registry Office, that it came to him that here was his last chance of getting them. Once past the Park Hotel, moving westward, you are in the desert.

He went in, and sank gratefully on to a stool at the counter. And it was not five minutes later that Tipton Plimsoll, sighting the Park Hotel through the window of his cab, tapped on the glass.

'Hey!' he said to the driver, and the driver said: 'Hey?'

'Stop the machinery,' said Tipton. 'I'm getting off.'

It does not take a swift taxi more than about ten minutes to go from Barribault's to the Park Hotel, and this one of Tipton's had been exceptionally swift. But in ten minutes a strong man can easily rally from a shock and become himself again. As Tipton stood outside the Park Hotel, he was blushing hotly at the thought that he had left a cocktail untested simply because a face had happened to bob up and pop off again.

A dozen explanations of the face's coyness had now presented themselves, each a hundred times more plausible than the one which had first chilled him. It might suddenly have remembered an appointment, or a letter to post, or a telephone call to make, or — well, practically anything. The supposition that it had had no existence outside his imagination and was working in cahoots with E. Jimpson Murgatroyd was so absurd that it made him laugh — merrily, like the crackling of thorns under a pot. He was still chuckling as he reached the bar and pushed open the door.

Over the bar of the Park Hotel, as over that of Barribault's, there is a large mirror. And Tipton, directing a casual glance at this to see if his tie was straight, rocked back on his heels and stood spellbound. He had seen a face. And there was no getting away from it, it was the face of a young man who looked like a kindly gorilla.

IV

To say of anyone's heart that it stood still is physiologically inexact. The heart does not stand still. It has to go right on working away at the old stand, irrespective of its proprietor's feelings. Tipton's, though he would scarcely have believed you if you had told him so, continued to beat. But the illusion that it had downed tools was extraordinarily vivid.

His eyes came out of his head like a snail's, and once more, as had happened at Barribault's, there swept over him the thought that E. Jimpson Murgatroyd, though not a man he liked or would ever invite to become his companion on a tour round the night clubs, was there with his hair in a braid as a prophet or tipster. 'Uncanny' was the word that suggested itself as descriptive of the fellow's flair for predicting the future. For the space of about thirty seconds Tipton's attitude towards E. J. Murgatroyd was that of a reverent savage towards the tribal medicine man.

This being so, it may seem strange that a mere couple of minutes later he was back to his original view that the Sage of Harley Street was a poor fish, a wet smack, and a mere talker through the hat.

But what happened was that at the end of these thirty seconds he closed his eyes, kept them closed while he counted a hundred, and then opened them. And, when he did so, the face had vanished. Not a trace of it anywhere.

A profound relief stole over Tipton, accompanied by the above-mentioned hard thoughts regarding E. J. Murgatroyd, and the explanation of the whole unpleasant episode presented itself to him. He saw now what must have occurred. His experience at Barribault's had hit him harder than he had supposed, inducing a form of auto-hypnosis and causing him to fall a ready victim to some trick of the light. His spirits, which had been low, soared to new heights. From feeling like thirty cents he snapped back to the old level of a million dollars. It was with a cheery breeziness which seemed to bring the sunshine streaming into the bar that he pranced to the counter and opened negotiations with the man behind it.

Sipping his second, he mentioned to the

barman that he was due at the Brompton Road Registry Office shortly and would be glad of a few words of advice from a friendly native as to how to get there. The barman said that that would be in Beaumont Street, and Tipton said 'Would it?' and the barman said it certainly would, and with the aid of a cherry and two cocktail sticks showed him how to set his course. Tipton thanked him with the sunny warmth which was endearing him to one and all this morning and went out, balancing the sticks and the cherry on the palm of his hand.

It was at about the same moment that Bill, who had found himself, even after his refreshment, too nervous to go on sitting at bars and had come out and started prowling feverishly up and down the Brompton Road, looked at his watch and decided that it was now time for him to go to the registry office and park himself in its waiting-room. It would never do for Prudence to arrive and find him missing. He turned eastward without delay.

The result was that Tipton, walking westward, got an excellent view of him just as he was about to turn into Beaumont Street, and his heart, after doing a few steps of a buck-and-wing dance, once more gave that illusion of standing still.

Adopting his old and tried policy, he closed his eyes. History repeated itself. When he opened them, the face had disappeared.

A few minutes earlier a similar occurrence had encouraged Tipton and calmed his fluttering nerves, but now it brought him no comfort whatsoever. It had become plain to him that this face which had suddenly come into his life was like the pea under the thimble — now you saw it and now you didn't — but it was always there or just lurking around the corner. This happened to be one of the occasions when it had melted into thin air; but it was a fat lot of good, he reflected very reasonably, faces melting into thin air, if they were going to come bobbing up again five minutes later. The vital fact which emerged was that, no matter to what extent this frightful face might play Peep-Bo, it was clearly from now on going to be his constant companion. The stuff, in short, had got him.

A sense of being unfairly discriminated against swept over Tipton Plimsoll. The aristocratic patient, of whom E. Jimpson Murgatroyd had spoken, had apparently abused his system fully as energetically as had he, Tipton, and yet, according to E. J. Murgatroyd, he had got off with a little man with a black beard, a phenomenon which Tipton felt he could have taken in his stride. You might in time, he felt, come to make quite a pet of a little man with a black beard. To be haunted by a face like the face which had begun to haunt him was a vastly different matter.

He was feeling very low now, low and despondent, and taking all the circumstances into consideration it seemed to him that the best thing to do was to step into the park and take a look at the ducks on the Serpentine. He had often found the spectacle of these agreeable birds act as a sedative in times of mental stress, soothing the soul and bringing new life and courage. And, indeed, there is always something very restful about a duck. Whatever earthquakes and upheavals may be afflicting the general public, it stands aloof from them and just goes on being a duck.

He stepped into the park accordingly, and after a period of silent communion with the gaggle that lined the water front, returned to his quest of Beaumont Street. He found it and its registry office without difficulty, and walked into the waiting-room. It was a small, stuffy apartment, occupied at the moment only by a young man of powerful build who was sitting staring before him in the stuffed manner habitual with young men on their wedding mornings. His back was towards Tipton, and a kindly impulse came over the latter to tap him on the shoulder and urge him to escape while the going was good.

As he moved forward to do so, the young man looked round.

The next thing of which Tipton was conscious was that he was out in the street and that he was being spoken to by a voice that sounded vaguely familiar. The mists cleared away, and he perceived Freddie staring at him censoriously.

'What do you mean, you're feeling extraordinarily well?' demanded Freddie. 'I never saw you looking mouldier, not even on the morning after that night at the Angry Cheese, when you threw the soft-boiled eggs at the electric fan. You're crazy if you don't come to Blandings, Tippy.'

Tipton Plimsoll reached out a feeble hand and

patted him on the arm.

'It's all right, Freddie o' man. I am coming to Blandings.'

'You are?'

'Yessir, I can't get there quick enough. And I should be glad if while I am in residence, you would see that no alcoholic fluid of any description is served to me. I mean this, Freddie o' man. I have seen the light.' He paused for a moment with a quick shudder, remembering what else he had seen. 'And now excuse me. I have to go and look at the ducks on the Serpentine.'

'Why do you want to look at the ducks on the Serpentine?'

'There are moments in a man's life, Freddie o' fellow,' said Tipton gravely, 'when he has got to look at the ducks on the Serpentine. And about that lunch of ours. Cancel it. I'm going to lunch quietly at Barribault's on a rusk and a glass of milk. Pick me up there in the car when you're ready to start,' said Tipton, and walked off with bowed head.

Freddie, having followed his retreating form with a perplexed monocle till it was out of sight, turned and went into the registry office, where Bill was still sitting staring dully at nothing.

V

Into the early stages of the meeting between Frederick Threepwood and William Lister it is not necessary for the chronicler to go with any wealth of detail. It will be enough to say that they got together and picked up the threads. Few things are more affecting than these reunions of old buddies after long separation, but they involve too many queries as to what old What's-his-name is doing now and whatever became of old So-and-so to make good general reading.

We may pass, accordingly, to the moment when Bill, who had been rather less wholeheartedly absorbed in the fate of these once-familiar figures than his companion, looked at his watch and hazarded the suggestion that it was about time, surely, that the other contracting party to these proceedings showed up.

And Freddie, noting that the hands of the clock on the mantelpiece were now indicating half-past twelve, was forced to agree that his cousin's failure to put in an appearance was not unrummy. One expects on these occasions that the bride, like a heavyweight champion defending his title, will let the groom get into the ring first, but Prudence should certainly have been here by now.

Bill, whose nerves for the last hour or so had been sticking out of his body, twisting themselves about like snakes and getting all knotted at the ends, took a grave view of the matter. Having gasped for air once or twice, he put his apprehensions into words.

'Oh, gosh, you don't think she can have changed her mind?'

'My dear Blister!'

'She may have done.'

'Not a chance. I saw her this morning, and she was all in favour of the binge.'

'When was that?'

'Around about nine-thirty.'

'Three hours ago. Loads of time for her to have thought things over and decided to back out. As a matter of fact, I was rather expecting this. I've never been able to understand what she saw in me.'

'Tut, tut, Blister, this is mere weakness. Yours is a sterling character. I don't know a man I respect more.'

'I dare say, but look at my face.'

'I am looking at your face, Blister, and it's a fine, open, honest face. Not beautiful, perhaps, but what is beauty, after all? Skin deep, and you can quote me as saying so. Summing up, I consider that an undersized little half-pint like Prue is lucky to get such a mate.'

'Don't call her a half-pint!'

'Well, don't you be so dashed grovelling about her. She isn't the Queen of Sheba.'

'Yes, she is.'

'Pardon me.'

'Well, just as good, anyway.'

The thought came to Freddie that he had perhaps taken the wrong line in his endeavour to soothe and encourage. A silence fell, during which he sucked the knob of his umbrella thoughtfully while Bill, who had leaped from his chair as if it had been drawn to his attention that it was red hot, paced the room feverishly.

It was some moments before Freddie spoke.

When he did there was a touch of diffidence in his manner.

'Here's a thought, Blister. Could someone have been telling her things about you?'

'How do you mean?'

'People do tell girls things about people. Some silly ass went and told Aggie I had once been engaged to my cousin Veronica, and I've never really heard the last of it since. Aggie is the sweetest girl in the world — an angel in human shape, you might say — but she still allows the subject to creep into her conversation at times, and I'm really taking a big chance giving Vee even the simplest of pendants for her birthday. Somebody may have been telling Prue about your private life.'

'My what?'

'Well, you know what I mean. Artists are artists. Or so I've always heard. Nameless orgies in the old studio, and all that sort of thing.'

'Don't be a damned fool. My life has always been — '

'Clean?'

'You could eat your dinner off it.'

Freddie took another chew at the knob of his umbrella.

'In that case,' he said, 'my theory falls to the ground. It was only a suggestion, anyway. What do you make the time?'

'A quarter to one.'

'Then that clock's right. I'm afraid you must brace yourself to face the worst, Blister. It begins to look, I fear, as if she wasn't coming.'

'Oh, my God!'

'Let me think this over,' said Freddie, applying himself once more to the umbrella. 'There's only one thing to be done,' he resumed some moments later. 'I will pop round to Grosvenor Square and make enquiries. You, meanwhile, go and wait for me at Barribault's.'

Bill paled.

'Barribault's?'

'I've got to go and see a man there. I'm taking him down to Blandings this afternoon, and I want to make sure he's fit to travel. His manner, when I saw him not long ago, was strange. I didn't like the way he said he was going to lunch on a rusk and a glass of milk. It gave me the impression that he was merely wearing the mask and trying to lull my vigilance. Wait in the lobby till I come. I'll be as quick as I can.'

'Not in the lobby,' said Bill, with a reminiscent shiver. It was in the lobby, on his way from the dining-room to the main exit, that he had bumped into a small boy in buttons, who might have been the heir of some ruling house, and had been given one of those quick, sharp, searing looks which the personnel of Barribault's staff, however junior, always give to louts of outsiders who trespass on the hotel's premises. 'I'll be waiting in the street,' he said. It meant, of course, having to brave the scrutiny of the ex-King of Ruritania, but that could not be avoided.

Nervous strain has different effects on different people. It caused Bill, who always walked everywhere, to take a cab to Barribault's; whereas Tipton Plimsoll, who always took cabs

61

everywhere, decided to walk. The former, therefore, had already taken up his station at the entrance of the hotel when the latter arrived.

Bill, who was in a reverie, did not see Tipton. But Tipton saw Bill. He gave him a quick glance, then averted his eyes and hurried through the swing doors. The ex-King of Ruritania, touching his hat to him as he passed, noticed that his face was a rather pretty green and that he was shaking like a badly-set blancmange.

VI

When two men are isolated together in a confined space, it generally happens that the social barriers eventually break down and they start to fraternize. The ex-King of Ruritania's position of official stander on the sidewalk outside Barribault's Hotel was one of splendour and importance, but life tended when business was slack to become a little lonely for him, and at such times his prejudice against hobnobbing with the proletariat weakened.

It was not long, accordingly, before he had decided to overlook the bagginess of Bill's trousers and was telling him condescendingly that it was a nice day, and Bill, whose need for human sympathy had now grown acute, was replying that the day might be nice enough as far as weather conditions were concerned, but that in certain other vital respects it fell far short of the ideal.

He asked the ex-King if he was married, and

the ex-King said he was. Bill then said that he himself ought to have been by now, only the bride hadn't turned up, and the ex-King said that he doubted if a bit of luck like that would happen once in a hundred years. Bill had just asked the ex-King what he thought could have detained his betrothed, and the ex-King was offering to give him five to one that she had been run over by a lorry, when a cab whirled up, and Freddie stepped out.

Freddie's face was grave. He took Bill by the elbow and drew him aside. The ex-King, astounded that the latter should be on terms of intimacy with anyone so well dressed, gave his moustache a thoughtful twirl, said 'Coo!' and went on standing.

'Well?' said Bill, clutching at Freddie's arm.

'Ouch!' said Freddie, writhing like a tortured snake. Men of his companion's physique generally have a grip like the bite of a crocodile when stirred, and his conversation with the ex-King had stirred Bill a good deal.

'Did you see her?'

'No,' said Freddie, rubbing his sleeve tenderly. 'And I'll tell you why. She wasn't there.'

'Not there?'

'Not there.'

'Then where was she?'

'Bowling along in a cab on her way to Paddington.'

'Why on earth did she want to go to Paddington?'

'She didn't want to go to Paddington. She was sent there, with gyves upon her wrists, in the custody of a stern-faced butler, who had instructions from my aunt Dora to bung her into the twelve-forty-two for Market Blandings, first stop Swindon. The fact is, Blister, my poor dear old egg, you've rather gone and made a hash of things. A wiser man would not have rung her up at her home address and called her a dream rabbit, or, if he did, he would have taken the elementary precaution of ascertaining, before doing so, that he was speaking to her and not to her mother.'

'Oh, my God!'

'Naturally, Aunt Dora's suspicions were aroused. Prudence, interrogated, proved furtive and evasive, and the upshot was that Aunt Dora sought counsel of an even bigger hellhound than herself — my aunt Hermione, now in residence at Blandings. Aunt Hermione was on the telephone first thing this morning, advising her to wait till Prue took the dogs out for their after-breakfast airing. Those dogs,' said Freddie, 'have got rickets, or will have if they continue to eat Peterson's Pup Food. Peterson's Pup Food, I don't mind telling you, Blister, is a product totally lacking in several of the most important — Ouch!'

He paused, and released his biceps from the steely fingers which had once more become riveted to it.

'Get on, blast you!' said Bill, in a low, quivering voice. His demeanour was so menacing that Freddie, who had only touched the fringe of his critique of Peterson's degrading garbage, decided to postpone the bulk of his address to a more favourable moment. His companion was looking like a gorilla of testy and impatient habit from whom the keeper is withholding a banana. It would not have surprised Freddie greatly if he had suddenly started drumming on his chest with clenched fists.

'Of course, of course,' he said pacifically. 'I can quite understand your attitude. Naturally, you want the facts. In a nutshell, then, Aunt Hermione advised Aunt Dora to wait till Prue had popped out with the dumb chums and then go through her effects for possible compromising correspondence. She did so, and it was not long before she struck a rich lode — a bundle of about fifty letters from you, each fruitier than the last, tied round with lilac ribbon. Prue, grilled on her return, was forced to admit that you and she were that way, and further questioning elicited the confession that you were a bit short alike on Norman blood and cash. Ten minutes later her packing had begun; Aunt Dora supervising, she weeping bitterly.'

Bill clutched his hair. For an artist's, it was on the short side, but a determined man can clutch at anything.

'Weeping? I'd like to strangle that woman.'

'Aunt Dora is tough stuff,' assented Freddie. 'But, at that, you ought to see my aunt Constance, my aunt Julia, and my aunt Hermione, of whom I spoke just now. So there you are. Prue is now on her way to Blandings. I ought to mention that all the younger generation of my family get sent to Blandings when they fall

65

in love with the wrong type of soul mate. It's a sort of Devil's Island. It seems only yesterday that I was trying to console my cousin Gertrude, who was in the cooler for wanting to marry a curate. And I'd have been sent to Blandings myself, when Aggie and I were walking out, only I happened to be there already. Yes,' said Freddie, 'they've slapped young Prudence in the jug, and what you are probably asking yourself is what's to be done about it.'

'Yes,' said Bill. This was the very question which had presented itself to his mind. He eyed his friend hopefully, as if awaiting some masterly exposition of strategy, but Freddie shook his head.

'It's no good looking at me like that, Blister. I have no constructive policy. You're making me feel the way my father-in-law does at conferences. You don't know my father-in-law, of course. He's a bird who looks like a Roman emperor and has a habit of hammering on the table during conferences and shouting: 'Come on, come on, now. I'm waiting for suggestions.' And I seldom have any. But I'll tell you what I have done. I remembered Prue telling me that you were Uncle Gally's godson, and I stopped off at a call box and phoned him to meet us here. If anyone can think of the correct course to pursue, it will be this uncle. A man of infinite resource and sagacity. We may expect him shortly. In fact,' said Freddie, as a cab came to a halt with a grinding of brakes, 'here, if I mistake not, Watson, is our client now.'

Assisted by the ex-King of Ruritania, a trim,

dapper, perky little gentleman in the middle fifties was emerging from the cab. He advanced towards them jauntily, his hat on the side of his head, a black-rimmed monocle gleaming in his right eye.

VII

'Hullo there, Bill,' he said. 'Come along in and tell me all about it. I gather from Freddie that you're in a bit of trouble.'

He shook him warmly by the hand, and the ex-King of Ruritania gaped dazedly. He was feeling that he must have got his sense of values all wrong. Although he had stooped to converse with Bill, he had not abandoned his original impression that he was one of the dregs, even going so far as to suspect him of being an artist; and here the young deadbeat was getting the glad hand and the beaming smile from no less a celebrity than the eminent Gally Threepwood in person. It shook the ex-King and made him lose confidence in his judgement. For Gally was one of the nibs, one of the lights of London, one of the great figures at whom the world of the stage, the race-course, and the rowdier restaurants pointed with pride. In certain sections of the metropolis he had become a legend. If Joe Louis had stepped out of a cab and shaken hands with Bill, the ex-King could not have been more impressed.

The Hon. Galahad Threepwood was the only genuinely distinguished member of the family of which Lord Emsworth was the head. Lord Emsworth himself had once won a first prize for pumpkins, and his pig, as we know, had twice been awarded the silver medal for fatness at the Shropshire Agricultural Show; but you could not say that he had really risen to eminence in the public life of England. But Gally had made a name for himself. There were men in London — bookmakers, skittle sharps, jellied eel sellers on race-courses, and men like that — who would have been puzzled to know whom you were referring to if you had mentioned Einstein, but they all knew Gally.

The chief thing anyone would have noticed about Galahad Threepwood in this, his fifty-seventh year, was his astounding fitness. After the life he had led, he had no right to burst with health, but he did. Even E. Jimpson Murgatroyd would have been obliged to concede that he was robust. Where most of his contemporaries had reluctantly thrown in the towel and retired to Harrogate and Buxton to nurse their gout, he had gone blithely on, ever rising on stepping-stones of dead whiskies and sodas to higher things. He had discovered the prime grand secret of eternal youth — to keep the decanter circulating and never to go to bed before four in the morning. His eye was not dimmed nor his natural force abated, his heart was of gold and in the right place, and he was loved by all except the female members of his family.

He led the way through the swing doors, the ex-King touching his hat forty times to the minute like a clockwork toy, and settled his little flock at a table in the lounge. After that first dazzling smile of greeting there had come upon him an air of gravity and intentness. Freddie had not told him much over the telephone, but he had told him enough to make it clear that a very serious hitch had occurred in the matrimonial plans of a young man whom he loved like a son. He had always been devoted to Bill. One of his earliest recollections was of drawing him aside at the age of ten, tipping him half a crown, and urging him in a confidential whisper to place it on the nose of Bounding Bertie in the two-thirty at Plumpton. And he had always been happy to remember that Bounding Bertie had romped home by three lengths at the very satisfactory odds of a hundred to eight.

'Now then,' he said, 'what's it all about?'

The statement which Freddie had made to Bill had been, as we have seen, admirably clear, omitting no detail, however slight. Repeated now, it impressed the facts with equal lucidity on the Hon. Galahad. He nodded intelligently from time to time as the narrative proceeded, and when it had wound to its conclusion made the comment that this was a nice bit of box fruit. And both Bill and Freddie agreed with him.

'Shipped her off to Blandings, have they?' said the Hon. Galahad, removing his eyeglass and polishing it meditatively. 'The old, old story, by gad. Years ago, before either of you kids was born, they shipped me off to Blandings, to stop me marrying a girl on the halls named Dolly Henderson.' He sat for a moment, his eyes dreamy, his thoughts in the past. He had touched briefly on the tragedy of his life. Then he gave himself a little shake and returned to the present. 'Well, it's obvious what you must do, Bill. Can't leave the poor child crying her eyes out, alone in the middle of a pack of wild aunts. You'll have to go to Blandings too.'

Freddie, great though his respect was for his gifted relative, shook his head dubiously.

'But, dash it, Uncle Gally, they'll give him the bum's rush the instant he sets foot inside the door.'

'Who said anything about setting feet inside doors? I see I haven't made myself clear. I shouldn't have said 'Blandings'. What I meant was 'Market Blandings'. You book a ticket to Market Blandings, Bill, and establish yourself at the Emsworth Arms. You'll like the Emsworth Arms. Good beer. I wonder if they've still got the same potboy they had last summer. Nice chap. Name of 'Erbert. Great friend of mine. No side about him. If he's there, give him my love.'

Freddie was still groping.

'I don't get it yet. What's Blister supposed to do at the Emsworth Arms?'

'Merely make it his headquarters. Got to sleep somewhere, hasn't he? During the day he'll be up at the castle, of course, painting the pig.'

'Painting the pig?'

'Ah yes, I should have explained. I ought to have mentioned that your aunt Dora informed me the other day that your father had written to her, asking her to get him an artist to paint the portrait of his pig.'

'Gosh!' said Bill, light beginning to dawn.

70

4

I

To travel from Paddington to Market Blandings takes a fast train about three hours and forty minutes. Prudence Garland, duly bunged into the twelve-forty-two by her mother's butler, reached her destination shortly before five, in nice time for a cup of tea and a good cry.

A prospective bride, torn from her betrothed on her wedding morning, is seldom really lively company, and Prudence provided no exception to this generalization. Tipton Plimsoll, now violently prejudiced against Bill Lister's face, might have wondered why anyone should be fussy about not being allowed to marry a man with such a map, but she could not see it that way. She made no secret of the fact that she viewed the situation with concern, and her deportment from the start would have cast a shadow on a Parisian Four Arts Ball.

It is not surprising, therefore, that Tipton's first impression of the ancient home of the Emsworths, when he arrived an hour or so later in the car with Freddie, should have been one of melancholy. Even though Prudence was absent at the moment, having taken her broken heart out for an airing in the grounds, an atmosphere of doom and gloom still pervaded the premises like the smell of boiling cabbage. Tipton was not acquainted with the writings of Edgar Allan Poe, and so had never heard of the House of Usher, but a more widely read man in his place might well have supposed himself to have crossed the threshold of that rather depressing establishment.

This note of sombreness was particularly manifest in Lord Emsworth. A kind-hearted man, he was always vaguely pained when one of his numerous nieces came to serve her sentence at Blandings for having loved not wisely but too well; and in addition to this, almost the first of Prudence's broken utterances, as she toyed with her tea and muffins, had been the announcement that, life being now a blank for her, she proposed to devote herself to the doing of good works.

He knew what that meant. It meant that his study was going to be tidied again. True, all the stricken girl had actually said, was that she intended to interest herself in the Infants' Bible Class down in Blandings Parva, but he knew the thing would go deeper than that. From superintending an Infants' Bible Class to becoming a Little Mother and tidying studies is but a step.

His niece Gertrude, while doing her stretch for wanting to marry the curate, had been, he recalled, a very virulent study tidier; and he saw no reason to suppose that Prudence, once she had settled down and hit her stride, would not equal, or even surpass, her cousin's excesses in this direction. For the moment she might slake her thirst for good works with Bible classes, but something told Lord Emsworth that in doing so sight of her seemed to tap in him a new vein of brilliance.

It was he who led the liveliest sallies. It was he who told the raciest anecdotes. It was he who, in between the soup and fish courses, entertained the company with a diverting balancing trick with a fork and a wineglass. For a time, in short, he was the spirit of Mirth incarnate.

For a time, one says. To be specific, up to the moment of the serving of the entrée. For it was just then that the figures in the tapestries on the walls noted that a strange silence had fallen upon the young master of the revels and that he refused the entrée in a manner that can only be described as Byronic. Something, it was clear, had suddenly gone amiss with Tipton Plimsoll.

The fact was that, taking another of his rapt looks at Veronica, he had been stunned to observe her slap Freddie roguishly on the wrist, at the same time telling him not to be so silly, and the spectacle had got right in among his vital organs and twisted them into a spiral.

For some time he had been aware that these two had seemed to be getting along pretty darned well together, but, struggling to preserve the open mind, he had told himself that a certain chumminess between cousins had always to be budgeted for. This wrist-slapping sequence, however, was another matter. It seemed to him to go far beyond mere cousinly good will. He was a man of strong passions, and the green-eyed monster ran up his leg and bit him to the bone.

'No, thank you,' he said coldly to the footman

81

who was trying to interest him in chicken livers and pastry.

And yet, had he but known it, in what had caused Veronica to slap Freddie on the wrist there had been nothing to bring the blush of shame to the cheek of modesty. All that had happened was that Freddie had told her in a confidential undertone that a Donaldson's dog biscuit was so superbly wholesome as to be actually fit for human consumption. Upon which, as a girl of her mentality might have been expected to do, she had slapped him playfully on the wrist and told him not to be so silly.

But Tipton, not being in possession of the facts, writhed from stem to stern and relapsed into a dark silence. And this so concerned Lady Hermione that she sought for first causes. Following his sidelong glances, she understood the position of affairs, and registered a resolve to have a heart-to-heart talk with Freddie at the conclusion of the meal. She also promised herself a word with her daughter.

The latter of these two tasks she was able to perform when the female members of the party rose and left the men to their port. And so well did she perform it that the first thing Tipton beheld on entering the drawing-room was Veronica Wedge advancing towards him, a fleecy wrap about her lovely shoulders.

'Mummie says would you like to see the garden by moonlight,' she said, in her direct way.

A moment before Tipton had been feeling that life was a hollow thing, for on top of the spectacle of this girl slapping the wrists of other

IV

In moments of emotion Lord Emsworth's pince-nez always sprang from their base, dancing sportively at the end of their string. The sight of a stealthy figure emerging from the window of the drawing-room caused them to do so now, for he took it for granted that it must be that of a burglar. Then he reflected that burglars do not come out, they go in, and it was in a calmer frame of mind that he reached for the dangling glasses, hauled in the slack, and replaced them on his nose.

He then saw that the other was no midnight marauder, but merely his guest Popkins or Perkins or Wilbraham — the exact name had escaped his memory.

'Ah, Mr Er,' he said genially.

As a rule, the seigneur of Blandings Castle was not very fond of the society of his juniors. In fact, the only time he ever moved with any real rapidity and nimbleness was when endeavouring to avoid them. But to-night he was feeling a kindly benevolence towards the whole human species.

To this Prudence's change of heart had, of course, contributed, but it was principally owing to the fact that in the course of the conversation over the port his son Frederick had mentioned that this time he would not, as had always happened before, be sticking to Blandings Castle like a limpet on a rock, but rather using it simply as a base for operations in the neighbourhood. Shropshire and its adjoining counties are peculiarly rich in landowners with well-stocked kennels, and it was Freddie's intention to pay flying visits to these, sometimes staying the night, sometimes inflicting himself on his unfortunate prey for days at a time.

No father could help but be uplifted by such news, and Lord Emsworth's manner, as he proceeded, was very cordial and winning.

'Going out for a little walk, Mr Ah?' he said.

Tipton said that he was, adding in rather a defensive way that it was such a swell night.

'Beautiful,' agreed Lord Emsworth, and then, for he was a man who always liked to make his meaning quite clear, added, 'Beautiful, beautiful, beautiful, beautiful. There is a moon,' he went on, directing his young friend's attention to this added attraction with a wave of the hand.

Tipton said he had noticed the moon.

'Bright,' said Lord Emsworth.

'Very bright,' said Tipton.

'Very bright, indeed,' said Lord Emsworth. 'Oh, extremely bright. Are you,' he asked, changing the subject, 'interested in pigs, Mr Er — Ah — Umph?'

'Plimsoll,' said Tipton.

'Pigs,' said Lord Emsworth, raising his voice a little and enunciating the word more distinctly.

Plimsoll explained that what he had been intending to convey was that his name was Plimsoll.

'Oh, is it?' said Lord Emsworth, and paused awhile in thought. He had a vague recollection that someone had once told him to do something — what, he could not at the moment recall

— about someone of that name. 'Well, as I was about to say, I am just going down to the sty to listen to my pig.'

'Oh, yes?'

'Her name is Plimsoll.'

'Is that so?' said Tipton, surprised at this coincidence.

'I mean Empress of Blandings. She has won the silver medal in the Fat Pigs class at the Shropshire Agricultural Show twice — '

'Gee!'

' — in successive years.'

'Gosh!'

'A thing no pig has ever done before.'

'Well, I'll be darned.'

'Yes, it was an astounding feat. She is very fat.'

'She must be fat.'

'She is. Extraordinarily fat.'

'Yessir, I'll bet she's fat,' said Tipton, groaning in spirit. No lover, who has come out to walk in the moonlight and dream of the girl he adores, likes to find himself sidetracked on to the subject of pigs, however obese. 'Well, I mustn't keep you. You want to see your pig.'

'I thought you would,' said Lord Emsworth. 'We go down this path.'

He grasped Tipton's arm, but there was really no necessity for thus taking him into custody. Tipton had resigned himself to going quietly. He had had no experience in the difficult art of shaking off adhesive peers, and it was too late to start learning now. Merely registering a silent wish that his companion would trip over a moonbeam and break his neck, he accompanied him without resistance.

As usual at this hour, the Empress had retired for the night. It was only possible at the moment, accordingly, for Lord Emsworth to give his guest a mere word picture of her charms. But he held out the promise of better things to come.

'I will take you to see her to-morrow morning,' he said. 'Or, rather, in the afternoon, for I shall be busy in the morning arranging matters with this artist of Galahad's. My son Freddie,' he explained, 'tells me that my brother Galahad is sending down an artist to paint the Empress's portrait. It is an idea I have long had in mind. I wrote to my sister Dora, asking her to find me an artist, but she answered very rudely, telling me not to be absurd, and my sister Hermione was also opposed to the project. They seemed to dislike the idea of a pig appearing in the family portrait gallery. That was Hermione you sat next to at dinner. The girl sitting next to Freddie was her daughter Veronica.'

For the first time Tipton began to feel that something might be saved from the wreck of his moonlight walk.

'I thought she was very charming,' he said, limbering himself up for a good long talk on his favourite topic.

'Charming?' said Lord Emsworth, surprised, 'Hermione?'

'Miss Wedge.'

'I don't think I know her,' said Lord Emsworth. 'But I was speaking of my niece Veronica. A nice girl, with many good qualities.'

'Ah!' breathed Tipton reverently.

'She has an excellent heart, and seems fond of pigs. I saw her once go out of her way to pick up and drop back into the sty a potato which the Empress had nosed beneath the bars. I was very pleased. Not every girl would have been so considerate.'

Tipton was so overcome by this evidence of the pure-white soul of the goddess he worshipped that for a moment he was incapable of speech. Then he said 'Gosh!'

'My son Freddie, I remember, who was present — '

Lord Emsworth broke off abruptly. This third mention of his younger son had had the effect of stirring his memory. Something seemed to be coming to the surface.

Ah yes. He had it now. His bedroom . . . Egbert bursting in . . . himself jotting down that memorandum in his pig book.

'Freddie, yes,' he went on. 'Of course, yes, Freddie. I knew there was something I wanted to tell you about him. He and Veronica were once engaged to be married.'

'What!'

'Yes. It was broken off- why, I cannot at the moment recall — possibly it was because Freddie married somebody else — but they are still devoted to each other. They always were, even as children. My wife, I recollect, used to speak of Veronica as Freddie's little sweetheart. My wife was alive at that time,' explained Lord Emsworth, careful to make it clear this was no question of a voice from the tomb.

Although any possible misunderstanding had thus been avoided, Tipton's brow remained drawn and furrowed. Spiritually, he was gasping for air. At a boisterous reunion in a speakeasy someone had once hit him on the bridge of the nose with an order of planked steak. As he had felt then, so did he feel now. The same sensation of standing insecurely in a tottering and disintegrating universe.

Many lovers in his position might have consoled themselves with the reflection that Freddie, being now a married man, was presumably out of the race for Veronica Wedge's hand and heart. But Tipton had had the wrong sort of upbringing to permit of his drawing comfort from any thought like that. The son of parents who after marrying each other had almost immediately started marrying other people with a perseverance worthy of a better cause, his had been one of those childhoods where the faintly bewildered offspring finds himself passed from hand to hand like a medicine ball. And, grown to riper years, he had seen among his friends and acquaintances far too much of that Ex-Wife's Heart Balm Society Love Tangle stuff to be a believer in the durability of the married state.

That very Doris Jimpson, of whom he had once supposed himself enamoured, had become Doris Boole, Doris Busbridge, and Doris Applejohn in such rapid succession that the quickness of the hand almost deceived the eye.

So the fact that Veronica's little sweetheart was now a married man by no means seemed to

Tipton to render him automatically a non-starter. Freddie, he assumed, having wearied of Mrs Freddie, had sent her off to Paris to secure one of the divorces which that city supplies with such a lavish hand; and now, giving himself a preliminary shake preparatory to starting all over again, he was about to make a pass at his old love. That low-voiced remark of his at dinner, which had caused the girl to slap his wrist and tell him not to be silly, had, of course, been something in the nature of a sighting shot.

That was how Tipton summed up the situation, and while the moon did not actually go out with a pop, like a stage moon when some hitch occurs in the lighting effects, it seemed to him to have done so.

'I guess I'll be turning in,' he said hollowly. 'Getting kind of late.'

As he made his way back to the drawing-room, one coherent thought held sway in his seething mind; and that was that, faces or no faces, he had got to have a bracer. He was convinced that even E. J. Murgatroyd, had the facts been placed before him, would have patted him on the shoulder and bidden him go to it. He would never, Murgatroyd would reason, were he standing beside him now, need a drop of the right stuff more than at this shattering moment; and, after all, the clear-thinking medico would go on to point out, since two o'clock that afternoon he had been leading a quiet regular life, thus reducing risk to a minimum.

The decanter was still on the drawing-room table, fully half of its precious contents intact. To seize it and take a long, invigorating snort was with Tipton the work of an instant. Then, as a prudent man's will, his thoughts turned to the future. Owing to those insane instructions which he had given Freddie, that only non-alcoholic beverages should be served to him while at the castle, this, unless he took steps, was the last life-saver he would get till he returned to civilization. A prospect at which imagination boggled.

Swift action was required, and he acted swiftly. Hastening to his room, he found the large flask without which he never travelled, and which he had brought along this time partly from habit and partly out of sentiment. He took it down to the drawing-room and filled it. Then, feeling that he had done all that man could do to make the future safe, he returned to his bedchamber.

Probably owing to his prompt measures, the moon had now begun to shine again, and Tipton, leaning on the window sill looking down over the meadows and spinneys which it illuminated so tastefully, was sufficiently himself once more to regard its activities with approval. The fact that he was sharing the same planet with Freddie still aggrieved him, but he no longer feared the other as a rival. That gargle from the decanter had made him feel capable of cutting out a dozen Freddies, and it now occurred to him that a gargle from the flask might help the good work along still further.

He took one, accordingly, and was about to take another, when he suddenly checked the progress of hand towards his lips and leaned forward, peering. A moving something on the lawn below had caught his eye.

It seemed to be a human figure.

It was a human figure — that of Bill Lister, who had carried out his intention of walking to the castle and gazing up at Prudence's window. The fact that he had no means of knowing which of these many windows was hers in no way deterred him. He was planning to gaze up at them all and so make sure. And, as a matter of fact, he had made an extraordinarily accurate shot. Her room was next door to Tipton's, the one with the balcony.

He had been gazing up at it a moment before, and he now moved along and gazed up at Tipton's. And as the moonlight fell full on his face, Tipton shot backwards into the room, groped for the bed, and sank bonelessly upon it.

It was some minutes before he could nerve himself to return to the window and take another look. When he did so, the face was no longer there. Having appeared and leered, it had vanished. This, he now realized, was its set routine. He went back to the bed and sat down again, his chin on his hand, motionless. He looked like Rodin's Penseur.

★　★　★

Some little while later, Lord Emsworth, pottering upstairs to his bedroom, was aware of a long, thin form confronting him on the landing. A ghost, was his first impression, though he would have expected a White Lady or a man in armour with his head under his arm rather than a stringbean-like young man wearing horn-rimmed spectacles. Then, as had happened before, a little intensive blinking enabled him to identify the agreeable young fellow who had been so interested in pigs, his guest Mr Er or Mr Ah or possibly Mr Umph.

'Say,' said the apparition, speaking in a low, emotional voice, 'would you do me a favour?'

'You would like to listen to my pig again? It is a little late, but if you really — '

'Look,' said Tipton. 'Will you take this flask and put it away somewhere?'

'Flask? Flask? Flask? Eh? What? Put it away somewhere? Certainly, my dear fellow, certainly, certainly, certainly,' said Lord Emsworth, for such a task was well within his scope.

'Thanks,' said Tipton. 'Good night.'

'Eh? Oh, good night? Yes indeed,' said Lord Emsworth. 'Oh, quite, quite, quite.'

5

I

The Emsworth Arms, that old-world hostelry at which Bill Lister had established himself with his paints, brushes, canvas, easel, palette knives, and what not, stands in the picturesque High Street of the little town of Market Blandings; and towards the quiet evenfall of the third day after his arrival there a solitary two-seater might have been observed dashing up to its front entrance. The brakes squealed, a cat saved its life by a split second, the car stopped, and Freddie Threepwood alighted. Having given a couple of nights to the Cheshire Brackenburys, he was on his way to stay with the equally deserving Worcestershire Fanshawe-Chadwicks.

His visit to Cogwych Hall, Cogwych-in-the-Marsh, Cheshire, the seat of Sir Rupert Brackenbury, M.F.H., had left Freddie in a mood of effervescent elation. He had gone there with the intention of talking Sir Rupert into playing ball, and he had done so. His subtle sales talks had made this M.F.H. a devout convert to Donaldson's Dog-Joy. And when you bore in mind the fact that the initials M.F.H. stand for Master of Fox Hounds, you could see what that meant.

Chaps from neighbouring counties would

come to hunt with the Cogwych pack and be stunned by the glowing health of its personnel. 'Egad, Sir Rupert,' they would say, 'those hounds of yours look dashed fit.' To which Sir Rupert would reply, 'And no wonder, considering that they are tucking into Donaldson's Dog-Joy all the time, a bone-forming product peculiarly rich in Vitamins A, B, and C.' 'Donaldson's Dog-Joy, eh?' the chaps would say, and they would make a note to lay in a stock for their own four-leggers. And in due season other chaps would call on these chaps and say, 'Egad . . . ' Well, you could see how the thing would spread. Like a forest fire.

As he passed through the portal of the Emsworth Arms, he was whistling cheerily. Not the slightest presentiment came to him that he would find the affairs of Bill Lister in anything but apple-pie order. By this time the foundations of a beautiful friendship between Blister and the guv'nor should have been securely laid. 'Call me Uncle Clarence,' he could hear the guv'nor saying.

It was accordingly with a crushing bolt-from-the-blueness that the information which he received at the reception desk descended upon him. He had to clutch at a passing knives-and-boots boy to support himself.

'Leaving?'

'Yes, sir.'

'Leaving?' repeated Freddie incredulously. 'But, dash it, he's only just come. He was supposed to be here for weeks. Are you sure?'

'Oh, yes, sir. The gentleman has paid his bill,

and the cab is ordered for the six-o'clock train for London.'

'Is he in his room?'

'No, sir. The gentleman went for a walk.'

Freddie released the knives-and-boots boy, who thanked him and passed on. With pursed lips and drawn brows he returned to the two-seater. He was deeply concerned. Unless all the signs deceived him, something had gone seriously wrong with the works, and it was imperative, he felt, that he look into the matter without delay.

A promising line of enquiry occurred to him almost immediately, for the young men of Donaldson's Inc. are trained to think like lightning and it is seldom that they are baffled for more than about a minute and a quarter. If anyone could cast a light on this mystery, it would be his cousin Prudence. She surely must be an authoritative source. A man who has sweated four hours by train to a one-horse town in the country simply in order to be near the girl he loves does not, he reasoned, suddenly leg it back to where he started without a word of explanation to her.

A few moments later he was speeding on his way to the castle. No one could have been more acutely alive than he to the fact that this was going to be a nasty jar for the Worcestershire Fanshawe-Chadwicks, who would not get him quite so soon as they had expected, but that could not be helped. Into each life some rain must fall, and the Fanshawe-Chadwicks would have to stiffen the upper lip and stick it like men.

As Bill's patron and backer, duty called him to proceed to the fountain-head and obtain the low-down from the horse's mouth.

The two-seater was a car which could do seventy-five at the height of its fever, and he reached the castle gates in record time. But turning through them into the drive he slackened his speed. He had observed ahead of him a familiar figure.

He put a finger on the tooter and tooted a toot or two.

'What ho, Tippy!' he called. He was in a hurry, but one cannot pass an old buddy by with a mere wave of the hand after being away from him for two days.

Tipton Plimsoll stopped, looked over his shoulder, and, seeing who it was that had spoken, frowned darkly. For some little while he had been pacing the drive, deep in his thoughts. And among the thoughts he had been deep in had been several particularly hard ones relating to this tooting ex-friend.

Ex, one says, for where he had once beheld in Frederick Threepwood a congenial crony and a side-kick with whom it had been a pleasure to flit from high spot to high spot, he now saw only a rival in love, and a sinister, crafty, horn-swoggling rival at that, one who could be classified without hesitation as a snake. At least, if you couldn't pigeon-hole among the snakes bimbos who went about the place making passes at innocent girls after discarding their wives like old tubes of toothpaste, Tipton was at a loss to know into what category they did fall.

100

'Guk,' he said reservedly. A man has to answer snakes when they speak to him, but he is under no obligation to be sunny.

His gloom did not pass unnoticed. It could scarcely have done so except at a funeral. But Freddie, placing an erroneous interpretation upon it, was pleased rather than wounded. In a man who suddenly abstains from the alcoholic beverages which were once his principal form of nourishment a certain moodiness is to be expected, and all that this Hamlet-like despondency suggested to him was that his former playmate was still on the wagon, and he honoured him for it. His only comment on the other's bleakness of front was to lower his voice sympathetically, as he would have done at some stricken bedside.

'Seen Prue anywhere?' he asked, in a hushed whisper.

Tipton frowned.

'You got a sore throat?' he enquired with some asperity.

'Eh? No, Tippy, no sore throat.'

'Then why the hell are you talking like a suffocating mosquito? What did you say?'

'I asked if you had seen Prue anywhere.'

'Prue?' Tipton's frown deepened. 'Oh, you mean the squirt?'

'I don't know that I would call her a squirt, Tippy.'

'She looks like a squirt to me,' said Tipton firmly. 'Ruddy little midget.'

'She isn't a tall girl,' Freddie conceded pacifically. 'Never has been. Some girls are, of course, and some aren't. You've got to face it. Still, putting all that on one side for the nonce, do you know where I can find her?'

'You can't find her. She's gone with your aunt to call on some people named Brimble.'

Freddie clicked his tongue. He knew what these afternoon calls in the country were. By the time you had had tea and been shown round the garden and told how wonderful it had looked a month ago and come back to the house and glanced through the photograph album, it was getting on for the dinner hour. Useless, therefore, to wait for Prudence. Apart from anything else, there is a limit to the agony of suspense which you can inflict on Worcestershire Fanshawe-Chadwicks. You don't want to get the poor devils feeling like Mariana at the moated grange.

He performed complicated backing and filling manœuvres with the car. As he got its nose pointed down the drive, the idea struck him that Prudence might have confided in her cousin Veronica.

'Where's Vee?' he asked.

A quick tremor passed through Tipton Plimsoll. He had been expecting this. All that eyewash about wanting to see the squirt Prudence had not deceived him for an instant. The coldness of his manner became intensified.

'She went too. Why?'

'I just wanted a word with her.'

'What about?'

'Nothing important.'

'I could give her a message.'

'Oh, no, that's all right.'

There followed a silence, and it was unfortunate that during it Freddie should suddenly have recalled the powerful harangue which his aunt Hermione had delivered in the drawing-room after dinner on the night of his arrival. He saw now that he had come near to missing an opportunity of speaking the word in season.

In disembowelling her nephew on the occasion referred to, Lady Hermione Wedge had made it abundantly clear to him that the idea of a union between Tipton Plimsoll and her daughter was one that was very near her heart. And Freddie, considering the thing, had also been decidedly in favour of it. It would, he had perceived, fit in admirably with his plans if the man who owned the controlling interest in Tipton's Stores should marry a wife who could be relied on to use her influence to promote the interests of Donaldson's dog biscuits. And he knew that good old Vee, who had practically written the words and music of *Auld Lang Syne*, could be trusted to do her bit. Wondering how he could have been so remiss as not to have strained every nerve to push this good thing along earlier, he now addressed himself to repairing his negligence, beginning by observing that Veronica, in his opinion, was a ripper and a corker and a topper and didn't Tipton agree with him?

To this, looking like Othello and speaking like a trapped wolf, Tipton replied: 'Yup.'

'Dashed attractive, what?'

'Yup.'

'Her profile. Lovely, don't you think?'

103

'Yup.'

'And her eyes. Super-colossal. And such a sweet girl, too. I mean as regards character and disposition and soul and all that sort of thing.'

A man trained over a considerable period of time to become lyrical about dog biscuits at the drop of the hat never finds any difficulty in reaching heights of eloquence on the subject of a beautiful girl. For some minutes Freddie continued to speak with an enthusiasm and choice of phrase which would have excited the envy of a court poet. There was deep feeling behind his every word, and it was not long before Tipton was writhing like an Ouled Nail stomach dancer. He had known, of course, that this human snake was that way about the girl he worshipped, but he had not suspected that the thing had gone so far.

'Well,' said Freddie, pausing at length, 'I must be getting along. I shall be back in a few days.'

'Oh?' said Tipton.

'Yes,' Freddie assured him. 'Not more than two or three at the outside.'

And having delivered these words of cheer, he trod on the self-starter and put the two-seater into first. It seemed to him, as he did so, that the gears were a bit noisy. But it was only Tipton Plimsoll grinding his teeth.

II

Better news awaited Freddie on his return to the Emsworth Arms. Bill Lister had come in from

104

his walk and was up in his room, packing. Taking the stairs three at a time, he burst in without formality.

Although at the moment of his entry all that was visible of his friend was the seat of his trousers as he bent over a suitcase, Freddie, though not a particularly close observer, had no difficulty in discerning that he stood in the presence of a man into whose life tragedy has stalked. The face which now looked up into his was one which harmonized perfectly with the trouser seat. It was the face, as the trouser seat had been the trouser seat, of a tortured soul.

'Blister!' he cried.

'Hello, Freddie. You back?'

'Just passing through, merely passing through. What's all this about your leaving, Blister?'

'I am leaving.'

'I know you're leaving. They told me downstairs. The point — follow me closely here — is why are you leaving?'

Bill placed an undervest in the suitcase like a man laying a wreath on the grave of an old friend and straightened himself wearily. He looked like a gorilla which has bitten into a bad coco-nut.

'I've got the push,' he said.

Deeply concerned, Freddie was nevertheless not particularly surprised. The possibility, even the probability, of something like this happening if he went away and ceased to keep the other's affairs under his personal eye had always been in his mind.

'I feared this, Blister,' he said gravely. 'I should have remained at your side to counsel and advise. What came unstuck? Didn't the guv'nor like the portrait?'

'No.'

'But surely you haven't finished it already?'

A flicker of life came into Bill's set face. He packed a pair of pyjamas with something approaching spirit.

'Of course I haven't. That's just what I tried to make him understand. So far it's the merest sketch. I kept telling the old blighter . . . Sorry.'

'Not at all. I know whom you mean.'

'I kept telling him that a portrait of a pig must be judged as a whole. But the more I tried to make him see it, the more he kept giving me the push.'

'Have you got it here?'

'It's on the bed.'

'Let's have a — My God, Blister!'

Freddie, hastening to the bed and gazing down at the canvas which lay upon it, had started back like one who sees some dreadful sight. He was now replacing his monocle in his eye, preparatory to trying again, and Bill looked at him dully.

'You notice something wrong too?'

'Wrong? My dear old bird!'

'Don't forget it's not finished.'

Freddie shook his head.

'It's no good taking that line, Blister. Thank heaven it isn't. One wouldn't want a thing like that to spread any further. What on earth made you depict this porker as tight?'

'Tight?'

'The pig I see here is a pig that has obviously

been on the toot of a lifetime for days on end. Those glassy eyes. That weak smile. I've seen old Tippy look just like that. I'll tell you what it reminds me of. One of those comic pigs you see in Christmas numbers.'

Bill was shaken. The artistic temperament can stand only just so much destructive criticism. He, too, approached the bed and examining his handiwork was compelled to recognize a certain crude justice in the other's words. He had not noticed it before, but in the Empress's mild face, as it leered from the canvas, there was a distinct suggestion of inebriation. Her whole aspect was that of a pig which had been seeing the new year in.

'That's odd,' he said, frowning thoughtfully.

'Worse than odd,' corrected Freddie. 'I don't wonder the guv'nor was stirred to his depths.'

'I think where I must have gone wrong,' said Bill, stepping back and closing one eye, 'was in trying to get some animation into her face. You've no notion, Freddie, how disheartening it is for an artist to come up against a sitter like that. She just lay on her side with her eyes shut and bits of potato dribbling out of the corner of her mouth. Velazquez would have been baffled. It seemed to me that I had somehow got to create a bit of sparkle, so I prodded her with a stick and shoved the result down like lightning before she could go to sleep again. But I see what you mean. The expression isn't right.'

'Nor the shape. You've made her oblong.'

'Oh, that's nothing. I should probably have altered that. I have been experimenting in the cubist form lately, and I just tried it as an idea. Purely tentative.'

Freddie looked at his watch, and was shocked at the position of the hands. Already the wretched Fanshawe-Chadwicks must be suffering agonies, which would inevitably become more and more severe. But he could not leave matters as they stood. He sighed and forced the picture of the Fanshawe-Chadwicks from his mind.

'Tell me exactly what took place, Blister. Up to a certain point, of course, I can visualize the scene. You at your easel, plying the brush; the guv'nor toddling up, adjusting his pince-nez. He stands behind you. He peers over your shoulder. He starts back with a hoarse cry. What then? Was what he proceeded to dish out undisguisedly the raspberry?'

'Yes.'

'No avenue was left open that might have led to a peaceful settlement?'

'No.'

'It would be no use your offering to rub it out and try again?'

'No. You see, I'm afraid I lost my temper a bit. I forget what I said exactly, but it was to the effect that if I had known he wanted the pretty-pretty, chocolate-box sort of thing, I would never have accepted the commission. That and something about stifling the freedom of expression of the artist. Oh yes, and I told him to go and boil his head.'

'You did? H'm,' said Freddie. 'Ha. 'Myes. Um. This isn't too good, Blister.'

108

'No.'

'Prue may be upset.'

Bill shuddered.

'She is.'

'You've seen her, then?'

Bill shuddered again.

'Yes,' he said, in a low voice. 'I've seen her. She was with your father, and she stayed on after he left.'

'What was her attitude?'

'She was furious, and broke off the engagement.'

'You astound me, Blister. You couldn't have understood her.'

'I don't think so. She said she never wanted to see me again, and was going to devote herself to good works.'

'To which you replied — ?'

'I hadn't time to reply. She streaked off like an electric hare, laughing hysterically.'

'She did, did she? Laughed hysterically, eh? The unbridled little cheese mite. I sometimes think that child is *non compos*.'

A look of menace came into Bill's strained face.

'Do you want your head bashed in?' he asked.

'No,' said Freddie, having considered the question. 'No, I don't think so. Why?'

'Then don't call Prue a cheese mite.'

'Don't you like me calling her a cheese mite?'

'No.'

'This would almost seem as if love still lingered.'

'Of course it lingers.'

'I should have thought you would have considered yourself well rid of a girl who hands you the mitten just because you failed to make a solid success of painting the portrait of a pig — an enterprise fraught, as you yourself have shown, with many difficulties.'

Bill quivered irritably.

'It wasn't that at all.'

'Then your story has misled me.'

'The real trouble was that she asked me to give up painting, and I wouldn't.'

'Oh, I see. You mean that pub business.'

'You know about that?'

'She told me that morning I met her in Grosvenor Square. She said you had inherited the Mulberry Tree, and she wanted you to run it as a going concern.'

'That's right. We've been arguing about it for weeks.'

'I must say I agree with her that you ought to have a pop at it. There's gold in them thar hills, Blister. You might clean up big as a jolly innkeeper. And as for giving up your art — well, why not? It's obviously lousy.'

'I feel that, now that I've had time to think it over. Seeing her leg it like that sort of opened my eyes. Have you ever seen the girl you love sprinting away from you, having hysterics?'

'No, now you mention it, I can't say I have. I've known Aggie to throw her weight about on occasion, but always in a fairly static manner. Unpleasant, I should imagine.'

'It does something to you, Freddie. It makes

110

you realize that you've been a brute and a cad and a swine.'

'I see what you mean. Remorse.'

'I'm ready now to do anything she wants. If she feels that I ought to give up painting, I'll never touch a brush again.'

'Well, that's fine.'

'I'm going to write and tell her so.'

'And have Aunt Hermione intercept the letter?'

'I never thought of that. Would she?'

'Unquestionably. When the younger female members of the family are sent up the river to Blandings, their correspondence is always closely watched.'

'You could slip her a note.'

'No, I couldn't. I told you I was merely passing through. I'll tell you what I will do, though. I'll nip up to the penitentiary now, and if Prue's got back, I'll place the facts before her. Wait here. I shan't be long. At least, I hope I shan't,' said Freddie, his mind sliding back to that painful vision of the Worcestershire Fanshawe-Chadwicks with their noses pressed against the windowpane and their haggard eyes staring yearningly out at an empty drive.

III

It was not so very long before Freddie once again presented himself in Bill's room, the latter's estimate of his absence at an hour and a half being erroneous and due to strained nerves.

111

In response to his friend's passionate complaint that there had been no need for him to stop by the roadside and make daisy chains, he waved a soothing hand.

'I've been as quick as was humanly possible, Blister,' he assured him. 'If I am late, it is merely because I was working in your interests. There were one or two little tasks I had to perform before I could return.'

'Is everything all right?'

'If you mean did I see Prue and square you with her, the answer is no. She hadn't got back from calling on some people she was calling on. The Brimbles, if you want to keep the record straight. They live out Shrewsbury way. Extraordinary, this rural practice of driving miles on a hot day to pay calls. You spend hours dressing in your most uncomfortable clothes, you tool across the countryside under a blazing sun, you eventually win through to Shrewsbury, and when you do, what have you got? The Brimbles. However,' proceeded Freddie, observing in his audience signs of impatience, 'you will want to know what steps I have taken, Prue being unavoidably absent. But before I slip you the lowdown, let me first get this thing straight. You really desire this reconciliation? I mean, in order to achieve it, you are prepared to creep, to crawl, to yield on every point?'

'Yes.'

'Realizing — I merely mention it in passing — that this will be a hell of a start for your married life, if and when reducing your chances

6

I

'Tchah!' said Colonel Wedge.

He spoke the word as it should be spoken, if it is to have its proper value, crisply and explosively from between clenched teeth. He had been sitting at the foot of his wife's bed, conversing with her while she breakfasted, as was his companionable habit of a morning. He now rose, and walking to the window stood staring out, jingling his keys irritably in his pocket.

'Good God! I never saw such a chap!'

Had there been some sympathetic friend standing at his side and following the direction of his moody gaze, such a one might have supposed the object of his remark to have been the gardener who was toying with a rake on the lawn below, and he would probably have felt the criticism to be fully justified. Nature has framed strange fellows in her time, and this was one of them, a gardener of vast physique and rendered more than ordinarily noticeable by the mustard-coloured beard of Assyrian cut which partially obscured his features.

It was not, however, to this fungus-covered son of the soil that the colonel alluded. He had seen him hanging about the place this last couple of days but had never given him more than a passing thought. When the heart is bowed down with weight of woe, we have little leisure for brooding on gardeners, however profusely bearded. The chap to whom he referred was Tipton Plimsoll.

There are fathers, not a few of them, who tend to regard suitors for their daughter's hand with a jaundiced and unfriendly eye, like shepherds about to be deprived of a ewe lamb. Colonel Wedge did not belong to this class. Nor was he one of those parents who, when their child has made an evidently deep impression upon a young millionaire, are content to sit back with folded hands and wait patiently for the situation to develop in a slow, orderly manner. He wanted action. He had observed the love light in Tipton Plimsoll's eyes, and what he wished to see in the fellow now was a spot of the Young Lochinvar spirit.

'What's he waiting for?' he demanded querulously, turning back to the bed. 'Anyone can see he's head over ears in love with the girl. Then why not tell her so?'

Lady Hermione nodded mournfully. She, too, was all in favour of dash and impetuosity. Looking like a cook who smells something burning, she agreed that the Plimsoll self-control was odd.

'Odd? It's maddening.'

'Yes,' agreed Lady Hermione, accepting the emendation. 'I don't know when I have been so upset. Everything seemed to be going so well. I'm sure it is affecting Veronica's spirits. She has not seemed at all herself these last few days.'

'You've noticed that? So have I. Goes into long silences.'

'As if she were brooding.'

'The exact word. She reminds me of that girl in Shakespeare who . . . How does it go? I know there's something about worms, and it ends up with something cheek. Of course, yes. 'She never said a word about her love, but let concealment, like a worm i' the bud, feed on her damned cheek.' Of course she's brooding. What girl wouldn't? Bowled over by a fellow at first sight; feels pretty sure he's bowled over too; everything pointing to the happy ending; and then suddenly, without any reason, fellow starts hemming and hawing and taking no further steps. It's a tragedy. Did I tell you what Freddie told me that day he arrived?' said Colonel Wedge, lowering his voice with the awe that befitted the revelation he was about to make. 'He told me that this young Plimsoll holds the controlling interest in one of the largest systems of chain stores in America. Well, you know what that means.'

Lady Hermione nodded, even more sadly than before — the cook who has discovered what it was that was burning, and too late now to do anything about it.

'And such a nice boy too,' she said. 'So different from what you led me to expect. Nothing could have been quieter and more correct than his behaviour. I noticed particularly that he had drunk nothing but barley water since he came here. What is it, Egbert?'

The solicitous query had been provoked by

the sudden, sharp cry which had proceeded from her husband's lips. Colonel Wedge, except for the fact that he was fully clothed, was looking like Archimedes when he discovered his famous Principle and sprang from his bath, shouting 'Eureka!'

'Good God, old girl, you've hit it. You've put your finger on the whole dashed seat of the trouble. Barley water. Of course! That's what's at the root of the chap's extraordinary behaviour. How the deuce can a young fellow be expected to perform one of the most testing, exacting tasks in life on barley water? Why, before I could work up my nerve to propose to you, I remember, I had to knock back nearly a quart of mixed champagne and stout. Well, this settles it,' said Colonel Wedge. 'I go straight to this young Plimsoll, put my hand on his shoulder in a fatherly way, and tell him to take a quick snort and charge ahead.'

'Egbert! You can't!'

'Eh? Why not?'

'Of course you can't.'

Colonel Wedge seemed discouraged. The fine, fresh enthusiasm died out of his face.

'No, I suppose it would hardly do,' he admitted. 'But somebody ought to give the boy a hint. Happiness of two young people at stake, I mean, and all that sort of thing. It isn't fair to Vee to let this shilly-shallying continue.'

Lady Hermione sat up suddenly, spilling her tea. She, too, looked like Archimedes — a female Archimedes.

'Prudence!'

'Prudence?'

'She could do it.'

'Oh, you mean young Prue? Couldn't think what you were talking about.'

'She could do it quite easily. It would not seem odd, coming from her.'

'Something in that. Prudence, eh?' Colonel Wedge mused. 'I see what you mean. Warm-hearted, impulsive girl . . . Devoted to her cousin . . . Can't bear to see her unhappy . . . 'I wonder if you would be offended if I said something to you, Mr Plimsoll.' . . . Yes, there's a thought there. But would she do it?'

'I'm sure she would. I don't know if you have noticed it, but Prudence has changed very much for the better since she came to Blandings. She seems quieter, more thoughtful and considerate, as if she were going out of her way to do good to people. You heard what she was saying yesterday about helping the vicar with his jumble sale. I thought that very significant.'

'Most. Girls don't help vicars with jumble sales unless their hearts are in the right place.'

'You might go and talk to her now.'

'I will.'

'You will probably find her in Clarence's study,' said Lady Hermione, refilling her cup and stirring its contents with a new animation. 'She told me last night that she was going to give it a thorough tidying this morning.'

II

'The stately homes of England,' sang the poetess Hemans, who liked them, 'how beautiful they

121

stand'; and about the ancient seat of the ninth Earl of Emsworth there was nothing, as far as its exterior was concerned, which would have caused her to modify this view. Huge and grey and majestic, flanked by rolling parkland and bright gardens, with the lake glittering in the foreground and his lordship's personal flag fluttering gaily from the topmost battlement, it unquestionably caught the eye. Even Tipton Plimsoll, though not as a rule given to poetic rhapsodies, had become lyrical on first beholding the impressive pile, making a noise with his tongue like the popping of a cork and saying: 'Some joint!'

But, as is so often the case with England's stately homes, it was when you got inside and met the folks that you saw where the catch lay. This morning, as he mooned morosely on the terrace, Tipton Plimsoll, though still admiring the place as a place, found himself not in complete sympathy with its residents. What a crew, he felt, what a gosh-awful aggregation of prunes. Tick them off on your fingers, he meant to say.

Lord Emsworth.............*A Wash-Out*
Colonel Wedge.............*A Piece of Cheese*
Lady Hermione...........*A Chunk of Baloney*
Prudence....................*A Squirt*
Freddie......................*A Snake*
Veronica Wedge...........

Here he was obliged to pause in his cataloguing. Even in this bitter mood of his, when he was feeling like some prophet of Israel judging the sins of the people, he could not bring himself to chalk up against the name of that lovely girl the sort of opprobrious epithet which in the case of the others had sprung so nimbly to his lips. She, and she alone, must be spared.

Not, mind you, but what he was letting her off a darned sight more easily than she deserved, for if a girl who could bring herself to stoop to a Frederick Threepwood did not merit something notably scorching in the way of opprobrious epithets, it was difficult to see what she did merit. And that she had fallen a victim to Freddie's insidious charms was clearly proved by her dejected aspect since his departure. You had only to look at her to see that she was pining for the fellow.

But the trouble was, and he did not attempt to conceal it from himself, he loved her in spite of all. King Arthur, it will be remembered, had the same experience with Guinevere.

With a muffled curse on his fatal weakness, Tipton made for the French windows of the drawing-room. It had occurred to him that the vultures which were gnawing at his bosom might be staved off, if only temporarily, by a look at the Racing Prospects in the morning paper. And as he approached them somebody came out, and he saw that it was the squirt Prudence.

'Oh, hullo, Mr Plimsoll,' said the squirt.

'Hello,' said Tipton.

He spoke with about the minimum of pleasure in his voice which was compatible with politeness. Never, even at the best of times, fond of squirts, he found the prospect of this girl's society at such a moment intolerable. And it is probable that he would have passed hurriedly on with some remark about fetching something from his room had she not fixed her mournful eyes upon him and said that she had been looking for him and wondered if she could speak to him for a minute.

A man of gentle upbringing cannot straight-arm members of the opposite sex and flit by when they address him thus. Tipton's 'Oh, sure,' could have been more blithely spoken, but he said it, and they moved to the low stone wall of the terrace and sat there, Prudence gazing at Tipton, Tipton staring at a cow in the park.

Prudence was the first to break a rather strained silence.

'Mr Plimsoll,' she said, in a low, saintlike voice.

'Hello?'

'There is something I want to say to you.'

'Oh, yes?'

'I hope you won't be very angry.'

'Eh?'

'And tell me to mind my own business. Because it's about Vee.'

Tipton removed his gaze from the cow. As a matter of fact, he had seen about as much of it as he wanted to see. A fine animal, but, as is so often the case with cows, not much happening. He found this conversational opening unexpectedly promising. His first impression, when this girl accosted him, had been that she wanted to touch him for something for the vicar's jumble sale, an enterprise in which he knew her to be interested.

'Ur?' he said enquiringly.

Prudence was silent for a moment. The rupture of her relations with the man she loved had left her feeling like some nun for whom nothing remains in this life but the doing of good to others, but she was wondering if she had acted quite wisely in so readily accepting the assignment which her uncle Egbert had given her just now. She had become conscious of a feeling that she was laying herself open to the snub of a lifetime.

But she did not lack courage. Shutting her eyes to assist speech, she had at it.

'You're in love with Vee, aren't you, Mr Plimsoll?'

A noise beside her made her open her eyes. Sudden emotion had caused Tipton to fall off the wall.

'I know you are,' she resumed, having helped to put him right end up again with a civil 'Upsy-daisy.' 'Anyone could see it.'

'Is that so?' said Tipton, in rather a nasty voice. He was stung. Like most young men whose thoughts are an open book to the populace, he supposed that if there was one thing more than another for which he was remarkable, it was his iron inscrutability.

'Of course. It sticks out like a sore thumb. The way you look at her. And what beats me is why you don't tell her so. She hasn't actually said anything to me, but I know you're making her very unhappy.'

Tipton's resentment faded. This was no time for wounded dignity. He gaped at her like a goldfish.

'You mean you think I've got a chance?'

'A chance? It's a snip.'

Tipton gulped, goggled, and nearly fell off the wall again.

'A snip?' he repeated dazedly.

'Definitely. To-day's Safety Bet.'

'But how about Freddie?'

'Freddie?'

'Isn't she in love with Freddie?'

'What an extraordinary idea! What makes you think so?'

'That first night, at dinner, she slapped his wrist.'

'I expect there was a mosquito on it.'

Tipton started. He had never thought of that, and the theory, when you came to examine it, was extraordinarily plausible. In the dining-room that night there had unquestionably been mosquitoes among those present. He had squashed a couple himself. A great weight seemed to roll off his mind. His eye rested for a moment on the cow, and he thought what a jolly, lovable-looking cow it was, the sort of cow you would like to go on a walking tour with.

Then the weight rolled back again. He shook his head.

'No,' he said, 'it was something he whispered to her. She told him not to be so silly.'

'Oh, that time, you mean? I heard what he said. It was about those dog biscuits of his being so wholesome that human beings could eat them.'

'Gosh!'

'There's nothing between Vee and Freddie.'

'She used to be engaged to him.'

'Yes, but he's married now.'

'Sure,' said Tipton, and smiled darkly. 'Married, yes. Married, ha!'

'And they were only engaged about a couple of weeks. I was at Blandings when it happened. It was raining all the time, and I suppose it was a way of passing the day. You get sick of backgammon. Honestly, I wouldn't worry about Vee being in love with other people, Mr Plimsoll. I'm sure she's in love with you. You should have heard her raving about that balancing trick you did at dinner with the fork and the wineglass.'

'She liked it?' cried Tipton eagerly.

'The way she spoke of it, I think it absolutely bowled her over. Vee's the sort of girl who admires men who do things.'

'This opens up a new line of thought,' said Tipton, and was silent for a space, adjusting himself to it.

'If I were you, I'd ask her to marry me right away.'

'Would you?' said Tipton. His eyes rested on Prudence and in them now there was nothing but affection, gratitude, and esteem. It amazed him that he could ever have placed her among the squirts. An extraordinarily bad bit of casting. What had caused him to do so, of course, had been her lack of inches, and he realized now that in docketing the other sex what you had to go by

127

was not size, but soul. A girl physically in the peanut division steps automatically out of her class if she has the opalescent soul of a ministering angel.

'Gosh!' he said. 'Would you?'

'I wouldn't waste another minute. Let me go and tell her that you want to see her, as you have something most important to say to her. Then you can put the thing through before lunch. Here is the set-up as I see it. I don't want to influence you if you have other ideas, but my suggestion would be that you ask her to come and confer with you behind the rhododendrons, and then, when she shows up, you reach out and grab her and kiss her a good deal and say: 'My woman!' So much better, I mean, than messing about with a lot of talk. You get the whole thing straight that way, right from the start.'

The motion picture she conjured up made a profound appeal to Tipton Plimsoll, and for some moments he sat running it off in his mind's eye. Then he shook his head.

'It couldn't be done.'

'Why not?'

'I shouldn't have the nerve. I'd have to have a drink first.'

'Well, have a drink. That's just the point I was going to touch on. I've been watching you pretty closely, and you haven't drunk anything since you got here but barley water. That's what's been holding you back. Have a good, stiff noggin.'

'Ah, but if I do, what happens? Up bobs that blasted face.'

'Face? How do you mean?'

128

Tipton saw that it would be necessary to explain the peculiar situation in which he had been placed, and he proceeded to do so. Looking on this girl, as he now did, as a sort of loved sister and knowing that he could count on her sympathy, he experienced no difficulty in making his confession. With admirable clearness he took her through the entire continuity — the acquisition of his money, the urge to celebrate, the two months' revelry, the spots, the visit to E. Jimpson Murgatroyd's consulting room, E. Jimpson's words of doom, the first appearance of the face, the second appearance of the face, the third, fourth, fifth, and sixth appearances of the face. He told his story well, and a far less intelligent listener than Prudence would have had no difficulty in following the run of the plot. When he had finished, she sat in thoughtful silence, staring at the cow.

'I see what you mean,' she said. 'It can't be at all pleasant for you.'

'It isn't,' Tipton assured her. 'I don't like it.'

'Nobody would.'

'It would be quite different if it were a little man with a black beard. This face is something frightful.'

'But you haven't seen it since the first night you were here?'

'No.'

'Well, then.'

Tipton asked what she meant by the expression 'Well, then,' and Prudence said that she had intended to advance the theory that the thing had probably packed up and gone out of business. To this Tipton demurred. Was it not more probable, he reasoned, that it was just lurking — simply biding its time as it were? No, said Prudence, her view was that, discouraged by Tipton's incessant barley water, it had definitely turned in its union card and that Tipton would be running virtually no risk in priming himself- within moderation, of course — for the declaration of his love.

She spoke with so much authority, so like somebody who knew all about phantom faces and had studied their psychology, that Tipton drew strength from her words. There was a firm, determined set to his lips as he rose.

'Okay,' he said. 'Then I'll have a quick snootful.'

He did not mention it, but what had helped to crystallize his resolution was the thought that in this matter of getting Veronica Wedge signed up, speed was of the essence. He had Prudence's assurance that the girl was still reeling under the effects of that balancing trick with the fork and the wineglass, but he was a clear-thinking man and knew that the glamour of balancing tricks does not last for ever. Furthermore, there was the menace of Freddie to be taken into account. His little friend had scouted the idea that there was any phonus-bolonus afoot between Veronica Wedge and this prominent Anglo-American snake, but though she had been convincing at the moment, doubts had once more begun to vex him, and he was now very strongly of the opinion that the contract must be sewed up before his former friend could return and resume his sinister wooing.

'If you'll excuse me,' he said, 'I'll pop up to my room. I've got a . . . No, by golly, I haven't.'

'What were you going to say?'

'I'd started to say I'd got a flask there. But I remember now I gave it to Lord Emsworth. You see, that time I saw this old face out of the window I kind of thought it would be better if somebody took charge of that flask for me, and I met His Nibs going to his room and gave it to him.'

'It's in Uncle Clarence's bedroom?'

'I guess so.'

'I'll go and get it for you.'

'Giving you a lot of trouble.'

'Not a bit. I was just going to tidy Uncle Clarence's bedroom. I've done his study. I'll bring it to your room.'

'It's darned good of you.'

'No, no.'

'Darned good,' insisted Tipton. 'White, I call it.'

'But I think one ought to help people, don't you?' said Prudence, with a faint, gentle smile like that of Florence Nightingale bending over a sick-bed. 'I think that's the only thing in life, trying to do good to others.'

'I wish there was something I could do for you.'

'You can give me something for the vicar's jumble sale.'

'Count on me for a princely donation,' said Tipton. 'And now I'll be getting up to my room. If you wouldn't mind contacting Miss Wedge and telling her to be behind the rhododendrons in about twenty minutes and bringing me the good old flask, you can leave the rest of the preliminaries to me.'

III

In the bearing of Tipton Plimsoll, as some quarter of an hour later he took up station at the tryst, there was no trace of the old diffidence and lack of spirit. He was jaunty and confident. The elixir, coursing through his veins, had given his system just that fillip which a lover's system needs when he is planning to seize girls in his arms and say, 'My woman!' to them. You could have described Tipton at this moment as the dominant male with the comfortable certainty of having found the *mot juste*. He exuded the will to win.

He looked at the sky sternly, as if daring it to start something. In the quick glance which he gave at the rhododendrons there was the implication that they knew what they might expect if they tried any funny business. He straightened his tie. He flicked a speck of dust off his coat sleeve. He toyed with the idea of substituting 'My mate!' for 'My woman!' but discarded it as having too nautical a ring.

A caveman, testing the heft of his club before revealing his love to the girl of his choice, would have shaken hands with Tipton in his present mood and recognized him as a member of the lodge.

Nevertheless, it would be falsifying the facts to say that beneath his intrepid exterior there did not lurk an uneasiness. Though feeling more like some great overwhelming force of nature than a mere man in horn-rimmed spectacles, he could not but remember that he had rather thrown down the challenge to that face. Far less provocation than he had just been giving it had in the past brought it out with a whoop and a holler, and Prudence's encouraging words had not wholly removed the apprehension lest it might report for duty now. And if it did, of course, phut went all his carefully reasoned plans. A man cannot put through a delicate operation like a proposal of marriage with non-existent faces floating at his elbow. Then, if ever, it is essential that he be alone with the adored object.

But as the minutes passed and nothing happened hope began to burgeon. His experience of this face had taught him that the one thing it prided itself on was giving quick service. That time in his bedroom, for instance, he had scarcely swallowed the stuff before it was up and doing. Nor had it been noticeably slower off the mark on other occasions. He could not but feel that this dilatoriness on its part now was promising.

He had just decided that he would give it a couple more minutes before finally embracing Prudence's theory that it had gone on the pension list, when a sharp whistle in his rear caused him to look around, and one glance put an end to his hopes.

On the other side of the drive, screening the lawn, was a mass of tangled bushes. And there it was, leering out from them. It was wearing a sort of Assyrian beard this time, as if it had just come from a fancy-dress ball, but he had no difficulty in recognizing it, and a dull despair seemed to crush him like a physical burden. Useless now to think of awaiting Veronica's arrival and going into the routine which Prudence had sketched out. He knew his limitations. With spectral faces watching him and probably giving him the horse's laugh to boot, he was utterly incapable of reaching out and grabbing the girl he loved. He turned on his heel and strode off down the drive. The whistling continued, and he rather thought he caught the word 'Hi!' but he did not look back. He could not, it appeared, avoid seeing this face, but it was some slight consolation to feel that he could cut it.

He was scarcely out of sight when Veronica Wedge came tripping joyously from the direction of the house.

Veronica, like Tipton five minutes earlier, was in excellent fettle. For the past few days she had been perplexed and saddened, as her father and mother had been, by the spectacle of an obviously enamoured suitor slowing down after a promising start. That moonlight walk on the terrace had left her with the impression that she had found her mate and that striking developments might be expected as early as the next day. But the next day had come and gone, and the days after that, and Tipton had continued to preserve his strange aloofness. And Melancholy was marking her for its own when along came Prudence with her sensational story of his wish to meet her behind the rhododendrons.

Veronica Wedge was, as has been indicated, not a very intelligent girl, but she was capable, if you gave her time and did not bustle her, of a rudimentary process of ratiocination. This, she told herself, could mean but one thing. Men do not lightly and carelessly meet girls behind rhododendrons. The man who asks a girl to meet him behind rhododendrons is a man who intends to get down to it and talk turkey. Or so reasoned Veronica Wedge. And now, as she hastened to the tryst, she was in buoyant mood. Her cheeks glowed, her eyes sparkled. A photographer, seeing her, would have uttered a cry of rapture.

A few moments later her animation had waned a little. Arriving at the rhododendrons and discovering that she was alone, she experienced a feeling of flatness and disappointment. She halted, looking this way and that. She saw plenty of rhododendrons but no Plimsoll, and she found this shortage perplexing.

However, she was not accorded leisure to brood on it, for at this point it was borne in upon her that she was not alone, after all. There came to her ears the sound of a low whistle, and a voice said 'Hi!' Assuming that this was her missing Romeo and wondering a little why he should have chosen to open an emotional scene in this rather prosaic manner, she spun around. And having done so she stood staring, aghast.

From out of the bushes on the other side of

the drive a bearded face was protruding, its eyes glaring into hers.

'Eeek!' she cried, recoiling.

It would have pained Bill Lister, the kindliest and most chivalrous of men, could he have read the *News of the World* headlines which were racing through her mind — FIEND DISMEMBERS BEAUTIFUL GIRL the mildest of them. Preoccupied with the thought of the note which he wished conveyed to his loved one, he had forgotten what a hideous menace the beard lent to his honest features. Even when clean-shaved, he was, as has been shown, not everybody's money. Peering out from behind Fruity Biffen's beard, he presented an appearance that might have caused even Joan of Arc a momentary qualm. But he had overlooked this. All he was thinking was that here at last was somebody who could oblige him by acting as a messenger.

His original intention had been to entrust the note to the tall, horn-rimmed spectacled chap who had been here a moment ago. He had seen him coming down the drive and, feeling that he looked a good sort who would be charmed to do a man a kindness, he had hurried across the lawn and intercepted him. And the fellow had merely given him a cold stare and proceeded on his way. Veronica's sudden appearance a few moments later had seemed to him sent from heaven. Girls, he reasoned, have softer hearts than men in horn-rimmed spectacles.

For a meeting with Prudence herself Bill had ceased to hope. If she sauntered about the grounds of Blandings Castle, it was not in the part of them in which he had established himself. And, in any case, the note put what he wanted to say to her so much more clearly and fluently than tongue could be trusted to do. He knew himself to be an unready speaker.

He wished he had some means of ascertaining this girl's name, for there was something a little abrupt in just saying 'Hi!' But there seemed no other way of embarking on the conversation, so he said it again, this time emerging from the bushes and advancing towards her.

It was most unfortunate that in doing so he should have caught his foot in an unseen root, for this caused him to come out at a staggering run, clutching the air with waving hands, the last thing calculated to restore Veronica's already shaken morale. If he had practised for weeks, he could not have given a more realistic and convincing impersonation of a Fiend starting out to dismember a beautiful girl.

'BLANDINGS CASTLE HORROR,' thought Veronica, paling beneath her Blush of Roses make-up. 'MANGLED BEYOND RECOGNITION. HEADLESS BODY DISCOVERED IN RHODODENDRONS.'

Daughter of a soldier though she was, there was nothing of the heroine about Veronica Wedge. Where other, tougher soldiers' daughters might have stood their ground and raised their eyebrows with a cold 'Sir!' she broke in panic. The paralysis which had been affecting her lower limbs gave way, and she raced up the drive like a blonde whippet. She heard a clatter of feet behind her; then it ceased and she was in sight of home and safety.

Her mother — a girl's best friend — was strolling on the terrace. She flung herself into her arms, squeaking with agitation.

IV

Bill went back to his lawn. There are moments in life when everything seems to be against one, and this was such a moment. He felt moody and discouraged.

Freddie had talked of smuggling a note to Prudence as if it were the easiest and simplest of tasks, and it was beginning to look like one calculated to tax the most Machiavellian ingenuity. And it was not as if he had got unlimited time at his disposal. At any moment some accuser might rise to confront him with the charge of being no genuine gardener, but merely a synthetic substitute.

This very morning he had thought that the moment had come, when Lord Emsworth had pottered up and engaged him in a lengthy conversation about flowers of which he had never so much as heard the names. And while he had fought off the challenge with a masterly series of 'Yes, m'lords' and 'Ah, m'lords' and once an inspired 'Ah, that zu zurely be zo, m'lord,' leaving to the other the burden of exchanges, could this happen again without disaster? His acquaintance with the ninth Earl of Emsworth, though brief, had left him with the impression that the latter's mind was not of a razor-like keenness, but would not even he, should another such encounter take place, become alive to the fact that here was a very peculiar gardener and one whose credentials could do with a bit of examination?

It was imperative that he find — and that, if possible, ere yonder sun had set — some kindly collaborator to take that note to Prudence. And where he had gone wrong, it seemed to him, had been in trying to enlist the services of horn-rimmed spectacled guests of the castle who merely glared and passed on, and neurotic females of the leisured class who ran like rabbits the moment he spoke to them. What he required, he now saw, was an emissary lower down in the social scale, to whom he could put the thing as a commercial proposition — one, for instance, of those scullions or what not of whom Freddie had spoken, who would be delighted to see the whole thing through for a couple of bob.

And scarcely had this thought floated into his mind when he espied coming across the lawn towards him a dumpy female figure, so obviously that of the castle cook out for her day off that his heart leaped up as if he had beheld a rainbow in the sky. Grasping the note in one hand and half a crown in the other, he hurried to meet her. A short while before he had supposed Veronica Wedge to have been sent from heaven. He was now making the same mistake with regard to her mother.

The error into which he had fallen was not an unusual one. Nearly everybody, seeing her for

139

the first time, took Lady Hermione Wedge for a cook. Where Bill had gone wrong was in his assumption that she was a kindly cook, a genial cook, a cook compact of sweetness and light who would spring to the task of assisting a lover in distress. He had not observed that her demeanour was that of an angry cook, whose deepest feelings have been outraged and who intends to look into the matter without delay.

Her daughter's tearful outpourings had left Lady Hermione Wedge so full of anti-bearded-gardener sentiment that she felt choked. The meekest mother resents having her child chivvied by the outdoor help, and she was far from being meek. As she drew near to Bill, her face was a royal purple, and there were so many things she wanted to say first that she had to pause to make selection.

And it was as she paused that Bill thrust the note and the half-crown into her hand, begging her to trouser the latter and sneak the former to Miss Prudence Garland, being careful — he stressed this — not to let Lady Hermione Wedge see her do it.

'One of the worst,' said Bill. 'A hellhound of the vilest description. But you know that, I expect,' he added sympathetically, for he could imagine that this worthy soul must have had many a battle over the roasts and hashes with Prue's demon aunt.

A strange rigidity had come upon Lady Hermione.

'Who are you?' she demanded in a low, hoarse voice.

'Oh, that's all right,' said Bill reassuringly. He liked her all the better for this concern for the proprieties. 'It's all perfectly on the level. My name is Lister. Miss Garland and I are engaged. And this blighted Wedge woman is keeping her under lock and key and watching her every move. A devil of a female. What she needs is a spoonful of arsenic in her soup one of these evenings. You couldn't attend to that, I suppose?' he said genially, for now that everything was going so smoothly he was in merry mood.

V

The soft-voiced clock over the stables had just struck twelve in the smooth, deferential manner of a butler announcing that dinner is served, when the sunlit beauty of the grounds of Blandings Castle was rendered still lovelier by the arrival of Freddie Threepwood in his two-seater. He had concluded his visit to the Worcestershire Fanshawe-Chadwicks. One assumes that the parting must have been a painful one, but he had torn himself away remorselessly, for he was due for a night at the Shropshire Finches. To look in at the castle en route he had had to make a wide detour, but he was anxious to see Bill and learn how he had been getting along in his absence.

A search through the grounds failed to reveal the object of his quest, but it enabled him to pass the time of day with his father. Lord Emsworth, respectably — even ornately — clad in a dark suit of metropolitan cut and a shirt with a stiff collar, was leaning on the rail of the pigsty, communing with his pig.

Accustomed to seeing the author of his being in concertina trousers and an old shooting jacket with holes in the elbows, Freddie was unable to repress a gasp of astonishment, loud enough to arrest the other's attention. Lord Emsworth turned, adjusting his pince-nez, and what he saw through them, when he had got them focused, drew from him, too, a sudden gasp.

'Freddie! Bless my soul, I thought you were staying with some people. Have you come back for long?' he asked in quick alarm, his father's heart beating apprehensively.

Freddie stilled his fears.

'Just passing through, Guv'nor. I'm due at the Finches for lunch. I say, Guv'nor, why the fancy dress?'

'Eh?'

'The clothes. The gent's reach-me-downs.'

'Ah,' said Lord Emsworth, comprehending. 'I am leaving for London on the twelve-forty train.'

'Must be something pretty important to take you up to London in weather like this.'

'It is. Most important. I am going to see your uncle Galahad about another artist to paint the portrait of my pig. That first fellow . . . ' Here Lord Emsworth was obliged to pause, in order to wrestle with his feelings.

'But why don't you wire him or just ring him up?'

'Wire him? Ring him up?' It was plain that Lord Emsworth had not thought of these

142

ingenious alternatives. 'Bless my soul, I could have done that, couldn't I? But it's too late now,' he sighed. 'I most unfortunately forgot that it is Veronica's birthday to-morrow, and so have purchased no present for her, and her mother insists upon my going to London and repairing the omission.'

Something flashed in the sunlight. It was Freddie's monocle leaping from the parent eye-socket.

'Good Lord!' he ejaculated. 'Vee's birthday? So it is. I say, I'm glad you reminded me. It had absolutely slipped my mind. Look here, Guv'nor, will you do something for me?'

'What?' asked Lord Emsworth cautiously.

'What were you thinking of buying Vee?'

'I had in mind some little inexpensive trinket, such as girls like to wear. A wrist watch was your aunt's suggestion.'

'Good. That fits my plans like the paper on the wall. Go to Aspinall's in Bond Street. They have wrist watches of all descriptions. And when you get there, tell them that you are empowered to act for F. Threepwood. I left Aggie's necklace with them to be cleaned, and at the same time ordered a pendant for Vee. Tell them to send the necklace to . . . Are you following me, Guv'nor?'

'No,' said Lord Emsworth.

'It's quite simple. On the one hand, the necklace; on the other, the pendant. Tell them to send the necklace to Aggie at the Ritz Hotel, Paris — '

'Who,' asked Lord Emsworth, mildly interested, 'is Aggie?'

'Come, come, Guv'nor. This is not the old form. My wife.'

'I thought your wife's name was Frances.'

'Well, it isn't. It's Niagara.'

'What a peculiar name.'

'Her parents spent their honeymoon at the Niagara Falls hotel.'

'Niagara is a town in America, is it not?'

'Not so much a town as a rather heavy downpour.'

'A town, I always understood.'

'You were misled by your advisers, Guv'nor. But do you mind if we get back to the *res*. Time presses. Tell these Aspinall birds to mail the necklace to Aggie at the Ritz Hotel, Paris, and bring back the pendant with you. Have no fear that you will be left holding the baby — '

Again Lord Emsworth was interested. This was the first he had heard of this.

'Have you a baby? Is it a boy? How old is he? What do you call him? Is he at all like you?' he asked, with a sudden pang of pity for the unfortunate suckling.

'I was speaking figuratively, Guv'nor,' said Freddie patiently. 'When I said, 'Have no fear that you will be left holding the baby,' I meant, 'Entertain no alarm lest they may shove the bill off on you.' The score is all paid up. Have you got it straight?'

'Certainly.'

'Let me hear the story in your own words.'

'There is a necklace and a pendant — '

'Don't go getting them mixed.'

'I never get anything mixed. You wish me to

have the pendant sent to your wife and to bring back — '

'No, no, the other way round.'

'Or, rather, as I was just about to say, the other way round. It is all perfectly clear. Tell me,' said Lord Emsworth, returning to the subject which really interested him, 'why is Frances nicknamed Niagara?'

'Her name isn't Frances, and she isn't.'

'Isn't what?'

'Nicknamed Niagara.'

'You told me she was. Has she taken the baby to Paris with her?'

Freddie produced a light blue handkerchief from his sleeve and passed it over his forehead.

'Look here, Guv'nor, do you mind if we call the whole thing off? Not the necklace and pendant sequence, but all this stuff about Frances and babies — '

'I like the name Frances.'

'Me, too. Music to the ears. But shall we just let it go, just forget all about it? We shall both feel easier and happier.'

Lord Emsworth uttered a pleased exclamation.

'Chicago!'

'Eh?'

'Not Niagara. Chicago. This is the town I was thinking of. There is a town in America called Chicago.'

'There was when I left. Well, anything been happening around here lately?' asked Freddie, determined that the subject should be changed before his progenitor started asking why he had

had the baby christened Indianapolis.

Lord Emsworth reflected. He had recently revised the Empress's diet, with the happiest results, but something told him that this was not the sort of news item likely to intrigue his younger son, who had always lacked depth. Delving into the foggy recesses of his mind, he recalled a conversation which he had had with his brother-in-law, Colonel Wedge, some half-hour earlier.

'Your uncle Egbert is very much annoyed.'

'What about?'

'He says the gardeners have been chasing Veronica.'

This startled Freddie and, though he was no prude, shocked him a little. His cousin Veronica, true, was a very alluring girl, but he would have credited the British gardener with more self-control.

'Chasing her? The gardeners? Do you mean in a sort of pack?'

'No, now I come to remember, it was not all the gardeners — only one. And it seems, though I cannot quite follow the story, that he was not really a gardener, but the young fellow who is in love with your cousin Prudence.'

'What!'

Freddie, reeling, had fetched up against the rail of the sty. Supporting himself against this, he groped dazedly for his monocle, which had once more become A.W.O.L.

'So Egbert assures me. But it seems odd. One would have expected him to chase Prudence. Veronica ran to your aunt Hermione, who immediately went to ask the man what he meant by such behaviour, and he gave her a letter and half a crown. That part of the story, also,' Lord Emsworth admitted, 'is not very clear to me. I cannot see why, if this man is in love with Prudence, he should have been conducting a clandestine correspondence with Hermione, nor why he should have given her half a crown. Hermione has plenty of money. Still, there it is.'

'If you'll excuse me, Guv'nor,' said Freddie, in a strangled voice, 'I'll be reeling off. Got some rather heavy thinking to do.'

He fished out the handkerchief again and once more applied it to his brow. The affair, perplexing to Lord Emsworth, held no element of mystery for him. For the second time, he saw, poor old Blister had gone and made a floater, putting the kibosh on the carefully-laid plans which had been devised for his benefit. The guv'nor had not mentioned it, but he assumed that the episode had concluded with his aunt Hermione slinging his unfortunate friend out on his ear. By this time, no doubt, the latter was in his room at the Emsworth Arms putting the finishing touches on his packing. But it was impossible to go there and confer with him. The delay involved would mean his being absent from the Finch luncheon table. And you cannot play fast and loose with Shropshire Finches any more than you can with Worcestershire Fanshawe-Chadwicks.

He passed slowly on his way, and he had not gone far before he beheld in front of him one of those rustic benches which manage to get themselves scattered about the grounds of country houses.

To a man whose mind is burdened with weight of care, rustic benches — *qua* rustic benches — make little appeal. He just gives them a glance and passes on, wrapped in thought. And this one would certainly not have arrested Freddie's progress had he not observed seated upon it his cousin, Veronica Wedge. And even as he gazed an emotional sniff rent the air and he saw that she was weeping. It was the one spectacle which could have taken his thoughts off the problem of Bill. He was not the man to stride heedlessly by when Beauty was in distress.

'Why, hullo, Vee,' he said, hurrying forward. 'Something up?'

A sympathetic listener, with whom she could discuss in detail the peculiar behaviour of Tipton Plimsoll in making assignations behind rhododendron bushes and then allowing her to keep them alone and be harried by wild gardeners, was precisely what Veronica Wedge had been wanting. She poured out her story in impassioned words, and it was not long before Freddie, who had a feeling heart, was placing a cousinly arm about her waist; and not long after that before he was bestowing on her a series of cousinly kisses. Her story being done, he gave her for her pains a world of sighs: he swore, in faith, 'twas strange, 'twas passing strange; 'twas pitiful, 'twas wondrous pitiful — at the same time kissing her a good deal more.

From behind a tree some distance away Tipton Plimsoll, feeling as if some strong hand

148

had struck him shrewdly behind the ear with a stuffed eelskin, stared bleakly at this lovers' reunion.

VI

Lord Emsworth reached London shortly before five, and took a cab to the Senior Conservative Club, where he proposed to book a room for the night. Bill, arriving in the metropolis at the same time, for he had travelled on the same train, made his way immediately to the headquarters of the Hon. Galahad Threepwood in Duke Street, St James's. From the instant when Lady Hermione Wedge, exploding like a popped paper bag, had revealed her identity, he had seen that his was a situation calling above all else for a conference with that resourceful man of the world. For though a review of the position of affairs had left him with the feeling that he was beyond human aid, it might just possibly be that the brain which had got Ronnie Fish married to a chorus girl in the teeth of the opposition of a thousand slavering aunts would function now with all its pristine brilliance, dishing out some ingenious solution of his problem.

He found the Hon. Galahad standing by his car at the front door, chatting with the chauffeur. An uncle's obligations were sacred to this good man, and he was just about to start off for Blandings Castle to attend the birthday festivities of his niece Veronica.

Seeing Bill, he first blinked incredulously, then

experienced a quick concern. Something, he felt, in the nature of a disaster must have occurred. To a mind as intelligent as his, the appearance in Duke Street of a young man who ought to have been messing about with a rake in the gardens of Blandings Castle could not fail to suggest this.

'Good Lord, Bill,' he cried. 'What are you doing here?'

'Can I have a word with you in private, Gally?' said Bill, with an unfriendly glance at the chauffeur, whose large pink ears were sticking up like a giraffe's and whose whole demeanour indicated genial interest and a kindly willingness to hear all.

'Step this way,' said the Hon. Galahad, and drew him out of earshot down the street. 'Now, then, what's all this about? Why aren't you at Blandings? Don't tell me you've made another bloomer and got the push again?'

'Yes, I have, as a matter of fact. But it wasn't my fault. How was I to know she wasn't the cook? Anyone would have been misled.'

Although still fogged as to what had occurred, the Hon. Galahad had no difficulty in divining who it was at Blandings Castle who had been taken for a cook.

'You are speaking of my sister Hermione?'

'Yes.'

'You thought she was the cook?'

'Yes.'

'Whereupon — ?'

'I gave her half a crown and asked her to smuggle a note to Prudence.'

'I see. Yes, I grasp the thing now. And she

150

whipped out the flaming sword and drove you from the garden?'

'Yes.'

'Odd,' said the Hon. Galahad. 'Strange. A precisely similar thing happened thirty years ago to my old friend Stiffy Bates, only he mistook the girl's father for the butler. Did Hermione keep your half-crown?'

'No. She threw it at me.'

'You were luckier than Stiffy. He tipped the father ten bob, and the old boy stuck to it like glue. It used to rankle with Stiffy a good deal, I remember, the thought that he had paid ten shillings just to be chased through a quickset hedge with a gardening fork. He was always a chap who liked to get value for money. But how did you happen to come across Hermione?'

'She came to tick me off for chasing her daughter.'

'You mean her niece.'

'No, her daughter. A tall, half-witted girl with goggly eyes.'

The Hon. Galahad drew his breath in sharply.

'So that was how Veronica struck you, was it? Yours is an unusual outlook, Bill. It is more customary for males of her acquaintance to allude to her as a goddess with the kind of face that launches a thousand ships. Still, perhaps it is all for the best. It would have complicated an already complicated state of affairs if there had been any danger of your suddenly switching your affections to her. But if the appeal she made to you was so tepid, why did you run after her?'

'I wanted her to take the note to Prue.'

151

'Ah, I see. Yes, of course. What was there in this note?'

'It was to tell her that I was ready to do everything she wanted — give up painting and settle down and run that pub of mine. Perhaps Freddie told you about that?'

'He gave me a sort of outline. Well, as far as the note is concerned, don't worry. I'm just off to Blandings. I'll see that she gets it.'

'That's awfully good of you.'

'Not at all. Is this it?' said the Hon. Galahad, taking the envelope which Bill had produced from an inner pocket like a rabbit from a hat. 'A bit wet with honest sweat,' he said, surveying it critically through his eye-glass, 'but I don't suppose she'll mind that. So you have decided to run the Mulberry Tree, have you? I think you're wise. You don't want to mess about with art these days. Hitch your wagon to some sound commercial proposition. I see no reason why you shouldn't make a very good thing out of the Mulberry Tree. Especially if you modernized it a bit.'

'That's what Prue wants to do. Swimming pools and squash courts and all that sort of thing.'

'Of course you'd need capital.'

'That's the snag.'

'I wish I could supply some. I'd give it to you like a shot if I had it, but I subsist on a younger son's allowance from the estate. Have you anyone in mind whose ear you might bite?'

'Prue thought Lord Emsworth might cough up. After we were married, of course. But the trouble is, I told him to boil his head.'

'And you were right. Clarence ought to boil his head. What of it?'

'He didn't like it much.'

'I still cannot see your point.'

'Well, don't you think it dishes my chance of getting his support?'

'Of course not. Clarence never remembers ten minutes afterwards what people say to him.'

'But he would recognize me when he saw me again.'

'As the chap who made a mess of painting his pig? He might have a vague sort of idea that he had seen you before somewhere, but that would be all.'

'Do you mean that?'

'Certainly.'

'Then why,' demanded Bill hotly, quivering with self-pity at the thought of what he had endured, 'did you make me wear that blasted beard?'

'Purely from character-building motives. Every young man starting out in life ought to wear a false beard, if only for a day or two. It stiffens the fibre, teaches him that we were not put into this world for pleasure alone. And don't forget, while we are on the subject, that it is extremely fortunate, as you happened to run into my sister Hermione, that you did wear that beard. Now she won't recognize you when she sees you without it.'

'How do you mean?'

'When you appear at the castle to-morrow.'

'When I — what?'

'Ah, I didn't tell you, did I? While we have been talking,' explained the Hon. Galahad, 'I have hit on the absurdly simple solution of your little problem. Clarence is coming to consult me about getting another artist to paint the Empress. He wired me from Market Blandings station that he would be calling here soon after five. When he arrives, I shall present you as my selection for to-day. That will solve all your difficulties.'

Bill gaped. He found it difficult to speak. One reverences these master minds, but they take the breath away.

'You'll never be able to get away with it.'

'Of course I shall. I shall be vastly surprised if there is the slightest hitch in the negotiations from start to finish. My dear boy, I have been closely associated with my brother Clarence for more than half a century, and I know him from caviare to nuts. His I.Q. is about thirty points lower than that of a not too agile-minded jellyfish. The only point on which I am at all dubious is your ability to give satisfaction for the limited period of time which must elapse before the opportunity presents itself for scooping Prudence out of the castle and taking her off and marrying her. You seem to have fallen down badly at your first attempt.'

Bill assured him that that was all right — he had learned a lesson. The Hon. Galahad said he hoped it was a drawing lesson. And it was at this moment that Lord Emsworth came pottering round the corner from St James's Street, and Bill, sighting him, was aware of a sudden access

154

of hope. The scheme which his benefactor had propounded called for a vague and woollen-headed party of the second part, and the ninth Earl of Emsworth unquestionably had the appearance of being that and more.

London, with its roar and bustle and people who bumped into you and omnibuses which seemed to chase you like stoats after a rabbit, always had a disintegrating effect on the master of Blandings Castle, reducing his mental powers to a level even below that of the jellyfish to which his brother had compared him. As he stood in the entrance of Duke Street now, groping for the pince-nez which the perilous crossing of the main thoroughfare had caused to leap from their place, his mouth was open, his hat askew, and his eyes vacant. A confidence man would have seen in him an excellent prospect, and he also looked good to Bill.

'Ah, here he is,' said Gally. 'Now follow me carefully. Wait till he comes up, and then say you've got to be getting along. Walk slowly as far as St James's Palace and slowly back again. Leave the rest to me. If you feel you want an excuse for coming back, you can ask me what it was I told you was good for the two o'clock at Sandown to-morrow. Hullo, Clarence.'

'Ah, Galahad,' said Lord Emsworth.

'Well, I must be getting along,' said Bill, wincing a little as the newcomer's pince-nez rested upon him. Despite his mentor's assurances, he could not repress a certain nervousness and embarrassment on finding himself once more face to face with a man with whom his previous encounters had been so painful.

His mind was still far from being at rest as he returned to Duke Street after the brief perambulation which he had been directed to make, and he found the cheery insouciance of the Hon. Galahad's greeting encouraging.

'Ah, my dear fellow,' said Gally. 'Back again? Capital. Saves me having to ring you up from the country. I wonder if you know my brother? Lord Emsworth, Mr Landseer.'

'How do you do?' said Lord Emsworth.

'How do you do?' said Bill uneasily. Once more he was feeling nervous and embarrassed. It would have been exaggerating to say that the ninth earl was directing a keen glance at him, for it was not within the power of the 'weak-eyed peer to direct keen looks, but he was certainly staring somewhat intently. And, indeed, it had just occurred to Lord Emsworth that some-where, at some time and place, he had seen Bill before. Possibly at the club.

'Your face seems familiar, Mr Landseer,' he said.

'Oh yes?' said Bill.

'Well, naturally,' said Gally. 'Dashed celebrated chap, Landseer. Photograph always in the papers. Tell me, my dear Landseer, are you very busy just now?'

'Oh no,' said Bill.

'You could undertake a commission?'

'Oh yes,' said Bill.

'Splendid. You see, my brother was wondering if he could induce you to come to Blandings with him to-morrow and paint the portrait of his

156

pig. You've probably heard of the Empress of Blandings?'

'Oh, rather,' said Bill.

'You have?' said Lord Emsworth eagerly.

'My dear chap,' said Gally, smiling a little, 'of course. It's part of Landseer's job as England's leading animal painter to keep an eye on all the prominent pigs in the country. I dare say he's been studying photographs of the Empress for a long time.'

'For years,' said Bill.

'Have you ever seen a finer animal?'

'Never.'

'She is the fattest pig in Shropshire,' said Gally, 'except for Lord Burslem, who lives over Bridgnorth way. You'll enjoy painting her. When did you say you were going back to Blandings, Clarence?'

'To-morrow on the twelve-forty-two train. Perhaps you could meet me at Paddington, Mr Landseer? Capital. And now I fear I must be leaving you. I have to go to a jeweller's in Bond Street.'

He shambled off, and Gally turned to Bill with pardonable complacency.

'There you are, my boy. What did I tell you?'

Bill was panting a little, like a man who has passed through an emotional ordeal.

'Why Landseer?' he asked at length.

'Clarence has always admired your Stag at Bay,' said the Hon. Galahad. 'I made it my talking point.'

7

I

The morning following Lord Emsworth's departure for London found Blandings Castle basking in the warmth of a superb summer day. A sun which had risen with the milk and gathered strength hourly shone from a sky of purest sapphire, gilding the grounds and messuages and turning the lake into a sheet of silver flame. Bees buzzed among the flowers, insects droned, birds mopped their foreheads in the shrubberies, gardeners perspired at every pore.

About the only spot into which the golden beams did not penetrate was the small smoking-room off the hall. It never got the sun till late in the afternoon, and it was for this reason that Tipton Plimsoll, having breakfasted frugally on a cup of coffee and his thoughts, had gone there to brood over the tragedy which had shattered his life. He was not in the market for sunshine. Given his choice, he would have scrapped this glorious morning, flattering the mountain tops with sovereign eye, and substituted for it something more nearly resembling the weather conditions of King Lear, Act Two.

It does not take much to depress a young man in love, and yesterday's spectacle of Veronica Wedge and Freddie hobnobbing on the rustic bench had reduced Tipton's vivacity to its lowest ebb. As he sat in the small smoking-room, listlessly thumbing one of those illustrated weekly papers for which their proprietors have the crust to charge a shilling, he was experiencing all the effects of a severe hangover without having had to go to the trouble and expense of manufacturing it. E. Jimpson Murgatroyd, had he beheld him, would have been shocked and disappointed, assuming the worst.

Nor did the periodical through which he was glancing do anything to induce a sprightlier trend of thought. Its contents consisted almost entirely of photographs of female members of the ruling classes, and it mystified him that the public should be expected to disburse hard cash in order to hurt its eyes by scrutinizing such gargoyles. The one on which his gaze was now resting showed three grinning young women in fancy dress — reading from right to left, Miss 'Cuckoo' Banks, Miss 'Beetles' Bessemer, and Lady 'Toots' Fosdyke — and he thought he had never seen anything more fundamentally loathsome. He turned the page hastily and found himself confronted by a camera study of an actress leering over her shoulder with a rose in her mouth.

And he was about to fling the thing from him with a stifled cry, when his heart gave a sudden bound. A second and narrower look had shown him that this was no actress but Veronica Wedge herself. What had misled him was the rose in the mouth. Nothing in his association with Veronica had given him the idea that she was a female Nebuchadnezzar.

There were unshed tears in Tipton's eyes as they stared down at this counterfeit presentment of the girl he loved. What a face, to sit opposite to at breakfast through the years. What a sweet, tender, fascinating, stimulating face. And at the same time, of course, if you looked at it from another angle, what a hell of a pan, with its wide-eyed innocence and all that sort of thing misleading honest suitors into supposing that everything was on the up and up, when all the while it was planning to slip round the corner and neck with serpents on rustic benches. So chaotic were Tipton Plimsoll's emotions as he scanned those lovely features with burning spectacles, that he would have been at a loss to say, if asked, whether he would have preferred to kiss this camera study or give it a good poke in the eye.

Fortunately, perhaps, he had not time to arrive at a decision on the point. A cheery voice said, 'Hullo, hullo. Good morning, good morning,' and he saw framed in the window the head and shoulders of a dapper little man in a grey flannel suit.

'Beautiful morning,' said this person, surveying him benevolently through a black-rimmed monocle.

'Grrh,' said Tipton, with the same reserve of manner which he had employed some days earlier when saying 'Guk' to Freddie Threepwood.

The newcomer was a stranger to him, but he

assumed from a recollection of conversation overheard at the breakfast table that he must be Veronica's uncle Gally, who had arrived overnight too late to mix with the company. Nor was he in error. The Hon. Galahad, having stopped at a roadside inn for a leisurely dinner and a game of darts, and subsequently having got into an argument with a local patriarch about the Corbett-Fitzsimmons fight, had reached the castle after closing time. This morning he had been rambling about in his amiable way, seeing the old faces, making the acquaintance of new ones, and generally picking up the threads. His arrival at the home of his ancestors always resembled the return of some genial monarch to his dominions after long absence at the Crusades.

'Hot,' he said. 'Very hot.'

'What?' said Tipton.

'It's hot.'

'What's hot?'

'The weather.'

'Oh,' said Tipton, his eyes straying back to the weekly illustrated paper.

'Regular scorcher it's going to be. Like the day when the engine driver had to get inside his furnace to keep cool.'

'What?'

'The engine driver. Out in America. It was so hot that the only way he could keep cool was by crawling into his furnace and staying there. Arising from that,' said the Hon. Galahad, 'have you heard the one about the three stockbrokers and the female snake charmer?'

Tipton said he had not — at least he made a strangled noise at the back of his throat which gave Gally the impression that he had said that he had not, so he told it to him. When he had finished, there was a silence.

'Well,' said Gally, discouraged, for a raconteur of established reputation expects something better than silence when he comes to the pay-off of one of his best stories, 'I'll be pushing along. See you at lunch.'

'What?'

'I said I would see you at lunch.'

'Guk,' said Tipton, and resumed his scrutiny of the camera study.

II

On the occasions of his intermittent visits to Blandings Castle, the mental attitude of the Hon. Galahad Threepwood, as has been said, resembled that of a genial monarch pottering about his kingdom after having been away for a number of years battling with the Paynim overseas; and like such a monarch in such circumstances what he wanted was to see smiling faces about him.

The moroseness of the young man he had just left had, in consequence, made a deep impression upon him. He was still musing upon it and seeking to account for it when he came upon Colonel Egbert Wedge, sunning himself in the rose garden.

As Gally always breakfasted in bed and the

colonel would have scorned to do anything so effete, this was the first time they had met since the banquet of the Loyal Sons of Shropshire, and their conversation for a few moments dealt with reminiscences of that function. Colonel Wedge said that in all his experience, which was a wide one, he had never heard a more footling after-dinner speech than old Bodger had made on that occasion. Gally, demurring, asked what price the one delivered half an hour later by old Todger. The colonel conceded that Todger had been pretty ghastly, but not so ghastly as Bodger. Gally, unwilling to mar this beautiful morning with argument, said perhaps he was right, adding that in his opinion both these territorial magnates had been as tight as owls.

A silence followed. Gally broke it by putting the question which had been exercising his mind at the moment of their meeting.

'Tell me, Egbert,' he said, 'who would a tall, thin chap be?'

Colonel Wedge replied truly enough that he might be anyone — except, of course, a short, stout chap, and Gally became more explicit.

'I was talking to him just now in the small smoking-room. Tall, thin chap with horn-rimmed spectacles. American, if I'm not mistaken. Oddly enough, he reminded me of a man I used to know in New York. Tall, thin, young, with a hell of a grouch and horn-rimmed spectacles all over his face.'

Colonel Wedge's eyebrows came together in a frown. He no longer found any difficulty in assisting the process of identification.

'That is a young fellow named Tipton Plimsoll. Freddie brought him here. And if you ask me, he ought to have taken him to a lunatic asylum instead of to Blandings Castle. Not,' he was obliged to add, 'that there's much difference.'

It was plain that the name had touched a chord in Gally's mind.

'*Tipton* Plimsoll? You don't happen to know if he has anything to do with a racket over in the States called Tipton's Stores?'

'Anything to do with them?' Colonel Wedge was a strong man, so he did not groan hollowly, but his face was contorted with pain. 'Freddie tells me he practically owns them.'

'Then that is why his appearance struck me as familiar. He must be the nephew of old Chet Tipton, the man I was speaking of. I seem to remember Chet mentioning a nephew. One of my dearest friends out there,' explained Gally. 'Dead now, poor chap, but when in circulation as fine a fellow as ever out-talked a taxi driver in his own language. Had one peculiar characteristic. Was as rich as dammit, but liked to get his drinks for nothing. It was his sole economy, and he had worked out rather an ingenious system. He would go into a speakeasy, and mention casually to the barman that he had got smallpox. The barman would dive for the street, followed by the customers, and there Chet was, right in among the bottles with a free hand. Colossal brain. So this young Plimsoll is Chet's nephew, is he? For Chet's sake, I am prepared to love him like a son. What's he grouchy about?'

Colonel Wedge made a despairing gesture.

'God knows. The boy's mentality is a sealed book to me.'

'And why do you say he ought to be in a loony bin?'

Colonel Wedge's pent-up feelings expressed themselves in a snort so vehement that a bee which had just settled on a nearby lavender bush fell over backwards and went off to bestow its custom elsewhere.

'Because he must be stark, staring mad. It's the only possible explanation of his extraordinary behaviour.'

'What's he been doing? Biting someone in the leg?'

Colonel Wedge was glad to have found a confidant into whose receptive ear he could pour the story of the great sorrow which was embittering the lives of himself, his wife, and his daughter Veronica. Out it all came, accompanied by gestures, and by the time he arrived at the final, inexplicable episode of Tipton's failure to clock in behind the rhododendrons, Gally was shaking his head in manifest concern.

'I don't like it, Egbert,' he said gravely. 'It sounds to me unnatural and unwholesome. Why, if old Chet had heard that there were girls in the rhododendrons, he would have been diving into them head foremost before you could say 'What ho.' If there is anything in heredity, I can't believe that it was the true Tipton Plimsoll who hung back on the occasion you mention. There's something wrong here.'

'Well, I wish you'd put it right,' said Colonel

165

Wedge sombrely. 'I don't mind telling you, Gally, that it's a dashed unpleasant thing for a father to have to watch his only child slowly going into a decline with a broken heart. At dinner last night Vee refused a second helping of roast duckling and green peas. That'll show you.'

III

As the Hon. Galahad resumed his stroll, setting a course for the sun-bathed terrace, his amiable face was wrinkled with lines of deep thought. The poignant story to which he had been listening had stirred him profoundly. It seemed to him that Fate, not for the first time in his relations with the younger generation, had cast him in the role of God from the Machine. Someone had got to accelerate the publication of the banns of Tipton Plimsoll and Veronica Wedge, and there could be no more suitable person for such a task than himself. Veronica was a niece whom, though yielding to no one in his recognition of her outstanding dumbness, he had always been fond, and Tipton was the nephew of one of his oldest friends. Plainly it was up to him to wave the magic wand. He seemed to hear Chet's voice whispering in his ear: 'Come on, Gally. Li'l speed.'

It was possibly this stimulation of his mental processes from beyond the veil that enabled him to hit upon a solution of the problem. At any rate, he was just stepping on to the terrace when his face suddenly cleared. He had found the way.

166

And it was at this moment that a two-seater came bowling past with Freddie at the wheel, back at the old home after his night with the Shropshire Finches. He whizzed by and rounded the corner leading to the stables with a debonair flick of the wrist, and Gally lost no time in following him. In the enterprise which he was planning he required the co-operation of an assistant. He found the young go-getter, his two-seater safely garaged and a cigarette in its eleven-inch holder between his lips, blowing smoke rings.

Freddie's visit to Sudbury Grange, the seat of Major R. B. and Lady Emily Finch, had proved one of his most notable triumphs. He had found Sudbury Grange given over to the damnable cult of Todd's Tail-Waggers' Tidbits, an even fouler product than Peterson's Pup Food, and it had been no easy task to induce his host and hostess to become saved and start thinking the Donaldson way. But he had done it. A substantial order had been booked, and during the drive to Blandings the exhilaration of success had kept his spirits at a high level.

But with the end of the journey, there had come the sobering thought that though his own heart might be light there were others in its immediate circle that ached like billy-o. Bill Lister's, for one. Prue's, for another. Veronica Wedge's, for a third. So now, when he blew smoke rings, they were grave smoke rings.

At the moment of Gally's appearance he had been thinking of Veronica, but the sight of his uncle caused Bill's unhappy case to supplant hers in the forefront of his mind, and he started to go into it without delay.

'Oh, hullo, Uncle Gally,' he said. 'What ho, Uncle Gally? I say, Uncle Gally, brace yourself for a bit of bad news. Poor old Bill — '

'I know, I know.'

'You've heard about him being given the bum's rush again?'

'I've seen him. Don't you worry about Bill,' said Gally, who believed in concentrating on one thing at a time. 'I have his case well in hand. Bill's all right. What we've got to rivet our attention on now, Freddie, my boy, is this mysterious business of young Plimsoll and Veronica.'

'You've heard about that too?'

'I've just been talking to her father. He seems baffled. You're a friend of this young Plimsoll. I am hoping that he may have confided in you or at least let fall something which may afford a clue to the reason for this strange despondency of his. I saw him for the first time just now, and was much struck by his resemblance to a rainy Sunday at a South Coast seaside resort. He is in love with Veronica, I presume?'

'All the nibs seem to think so.'

'And yet he takes no steps to push the thing along. Indeed, he actually gives her the miss in baulk when she goes and waits for him in the rhododendrons. This must mean something.'

'Cold feet?'

Gally shook his head.

'I doubt it. This young man is the nephew of my old friend Chet Tipton, and blood must surely tell. Chet never got cold feet in his life when there were girls around. The reverse, in fact. You had to hold him back with ropes. On the other hand, he did experience strange fits of despondency, when he would sit with his feet on the mantelpiece examining his soul. Another old friend of mine, Plug Basham, was the same. Very moody chap. However, I managed to snap Plug out of it, and I am inclined to think that the same method would be successful with this young Plimsoll. By great good luck we have the animal all ready to hand.'

'Animal?'

'Your father's pig. The worst attack of despondency from which I ever remember Plug suffering occurred when a few of us were at a house in Norfolk for the pheasants. We talked it over and came to the decision that what he wanted was a shock. Nothing serious, you understand, just something that would arrest his attention and take his mind off his liver. So we borrowed a pig from a neighbouring farm, smeared it with a liberal coating of phosphorus, and put it in his bedroom. It worked like magic.'

A certain concern had manifested itself in Freddie's aspect. His eyes bulged and his jaw dropped a little.

'You aren't going to put the guv'nor's pig in Tippy's bedroom?'

'I think it would be rash not to. They've given me the Garden Suite this time, with French windows opening on the lawn, so there will be no difficulty in introducing the animal. It almost seems as though it were meant.'

169

'But, Uncle Gally — '

'Something on your mind, my boy?'

'Would you really recommend this course?'

'It proved extraordinarily efficacious in Plug's case. He went into his room in the dark, and the thing caught him right in the eyeball. We heard a cry, obviously coming straight from the heart, and then he was pelting downstairs three stairs at a time, wanting to know what the procedure was when a fellow had made up his mind to sign the pledge — how much it cost, where you had to go to put in your application, did you need a proposer and seconder, and so forth.'

'But it might have worked the other way round.'

'I don't follow you.'

'What I mean is, if he'd been on the wagon already, it might have prompted him to take the snifter of a lifetime.'

'Plug wasn't on the wagon.'

'No, but Tippy is.'

Gally started. He was surprised and shocked.

'What? Chet Tipton's nephew a teetotaller?'

'Only in the past few days,' explained Freddie, who was the last man to wish to put a friend in a dubious light. 'Before that he was one of our leading quaffers. But after being on a solid toot for two months he has now signed off for some reason which he has not revealed to me, and at moment of going to press absorbs little except milk and barley water. It's a thing his best friends would have advised, and honestly, Uncle Gally, I doubt if you ought to do anything that might turn his thoughts back in the direction of the decanter.'

The Hon. Galahad's was a quick, alert mind. He could appreciate sound reasoning as readily as the next man.

'I see what you mean,' he said. 'Yes, I take your point. I'm glad you told me. This calls for a radical alteration in our plans. Let me think.'

He took a turn about the stable yard, his head bowed, his hands behind his back. Presently Freddie, watching from afar, saw him remove his monocle and polish it with the satisfied air of one who has thought his way through a perplexing problem.

'I've got it,' he said, returning. 'The solution came to me in a flash. We will put the pig in Veronica's room.'

A rather anxious expression stole into Freddie's face. Of the broad general principle of putting pigs in girls' rooms he of course approved, but he did not like that word 'we'.

'Here, I say!' he exclaimed. 'You're not going to lug me into this?'

The Hon. Galahad stared.

'Lug?' he said. 'What do you mean lug? The word 'lug' appears to me singularly ill-chosen. I should have supposed that as a friend of this young Plimsoll and a cousin of Veronica you would have been all eagerness to do your share.'

'Well, yes, of course, definitely, but I mean to say — '

'Especially as that share is so trivial. All I want you to do is go ahead and see that the coast is

171

clear. I will attend to the rough work.'

His words left Freddie easier in his mind. But that mind, what there was of it, was still fogged.

'But where's the percentage?'

'I beg your pardon?'

'What's the good of putting pigs in Vee's room?'

'My dear fellow, have you no imagination? What happens when a girl finds a pig in her room?'

'I should think she'd yell her head off.'

'Precisely. I confidently expect Veronica to raise the roof. Whereupon, up dashes young Plimsoll to her rescue. If you can think of a better way of bringing two young people together, I should be interested to hear it.'

'But how do you know Tippy will be in the vicinity?'

'Because I shall see to it that he is. Immediately after lunch I shall seek him out and engage him in conversation. You, meanwhile, will attach yourself to Veronica. You will find some pretext for sending her to her room. What pretext? Let me think.'

'She was threatening the other day to show me her album of school snapshots. I could ask her to fetch it.'

'Admirable. And the moment the starter's flag has dropped, give the gong in the hall a good hard bang. That will serve as my cue for unleashing young Plimsoll. I think we have synchronized everything?'

Freddie said he thought so.

'And the guv'nor being in London,' he pointed

out with some relief, 'you will be able to restore the animal to its sty without him knowing to what uses it has been put in his absence.'

'True.'

'A rather important point, that. Any funny business involving the ancestral porker is apt to wake the sleeping tiger in him.'

'Quite. That shall be attended to. One does not wish to cause Clarence pain. I suppose the best time to inject this pig would be after the gang have settled in at lunch. You won't mind being ten minutes late for lunch?'

'Try to make it five,' said Freddie, who liked his meals.

'And now,' said Gally, 'to find Prudence. I have a note to give her from Bill which, unless I am greatly mistaken, will send her singing about the premises like a skylark in summer. Where would she be, I wonder? I've been looking for her everywhere.'

Freddie was able to assist him.

'I met her in the village as I was driving through. She said she was going to see the vicar about his jumble sale.'

'Then I will stroll down and meet her,' said Gally.

With a parting instruction to his nephew to be on his toes the moment he heard the luncheon gong go, he sauntered off. His mood was one of quiet happiness. If there was one thing this good man liked, it was scattering light and sweetness, and to-day, it seemed to him, he was about to scatter light and. sweetness with no uncertain hand.

IV

Tipton Plimsoll stood on the terrace, moodily regarding the rolling parkland that spread itself before his lack-lustre eyes. As usual in this smiling expanse of green turf and noble trees, a certain number of cows, some brown, some piebald, were stoking up and getting their vitamins, and he glowered at them like a man who had got something against cows. And when a bee buzzed past his nose, his gesture of annoyance showed that he was not any too sold on bees either. The hour was half-past two, and lunch had come to an end some few minutes earlier.

It had proved a melancholy meal for Tipton. A light break-faster, he generally made up leeway at the midday repast, but on this occasion he had more or less pushed his food away untasted. Nothing in the company or the conversation at the board had tended to dispel the dark mood in which he had started the morning. He had been glad when the ritual of coffee-drinking was over and he was at liberty to take himself elsewhere.

His initial move, as we say, had been to the terrace, for he needed air and solitude. He got the air all right but missed out on the solitude. He had been looking at the cows for scarcely a minute and a quarter with growing disfavour, when a monocle gleamed in the sunshine and the Hon. Galahad was at his side.

Most people found Gally Threepwood a stimulating and entertaining companion and were glad of his society, but Tipton goggled at

174

him with concealed loathing. And when one says 'concealed', that is perhaps the wrong word. All through lunch this man had insisted on forcing upon him a genial flow of talk about his late Uncle Chet, and as far as Tipton was concerned Uncle Chet had reached saturation point. He felt that he had heard all that any nephew could possibly wish to hear about an uncle.

So now, starting away like some wild creature frightened by human approach, he was off the terrace and into the house before his companion could so much as be reminded of a story. The gloom of the small smoking-room drew him like a magnet, and he had fled there and was reaching out a limp hand for the weekly illustrated paper containing the camera study when the door opened.

'Aha!' said Gally. 'So here you are, eh?'

There is this to be said for the English country-house party, whatever its drawbacks, which are very numerous — when you have had as much of the gay whirl as you can endure, you can always do a sneak to your bedroom. Two minutes later Tipton was in his. And two minutes after that he found that he had been mistaken in supposing that he was alone at last. There was a knock on the door, the robust and confident knock of one who is sure of his welcome, and a dapper, grey-flannelled form sauntered in.

Anybody who wishes to be clear on Tipton Plimsoll's feelings at this juncture has only to skim through the pages of Masefield's *Reynard the Fox*. The sense of being a hunted thing was strong upon him. And mingled with it was resentment at the monstrous injustice of this persecution. If a country-house visitor is not safe in his bedroom, one might just as well admit that civilization has failed and that the whole fabric of society is tottering.

Agony of spirit made him abrupt.

'Say, you chasing something?' he demanded dangerously.

It would have required a dull man to be unconscious of the hostility of his attitude, and it did not escape Gally's notice that his young friend was rapidly coming to the boil. But he ignored the sullen fire behind the horn-rimmed spectacles.

'We do keep meeting, don't we?' he replied with the suave geniality which had so often disarmed belligerent bookmakers. 'The fact is, my boy, I want a long talk with you.'

'You just had one.'

'A long, intimate talk on a matter closely affecting your happiness and well-being. You are the nephew of my old friend Chet Tipton — '

'You already told me that.'

' — and I decline, I positively refuse to see Chet Tipton's nephew ruining his future and bunging golden prospects of roseate bliss where the soldier bunged the pudding, when I can put the whole thing right in half a minute with a few simple words. Come now, my dear fellow, we needn't beat about the bush. You love my niece Veronica.'

A convulsive start shook Tipton Plimsoll. His impulse was to deny the statement hotly. But even as he opened his mouth to do so, he found himself gazing at the lovely features of the camera study. Actually, the camera study was still in the small smoking-room, but he seemed to see it now, the rose dangling from its lips, and he had not the heart to speak. Instead, he gave a quick, low gulp like a bulldog choking on a piece of gristle, causing Gally to pat his shoulder five or six times in a fatherly manner.

'Of course you do,' said Gally. 'No argument about that. You love her like a ton of bricks. The whole neighbourhood is ringing with the story of your passion. Then why on earth, my dear chap, are you behaving in this extraordinary way?'

'What do you mean, extraordinary way?' said Tipton, weakly defensive.

'You know what I mean,' said Gally, impatient of evasion. 'Many people would say you were playing fast and loose with the girl.'

'Fast and loose?' said Tipton, shocked.

'Fast *and* loose,' repeated Gally firmly. 'And you know what the verdict of men of honour is on chaps who play fast and loose with girls. I have often heard your Uncle Chet express himself particularly strongly on the subject.'

The words 'To hell with my Uncle Chet' trembled on Tipton's lips, but he forced them back in favour of others more germane to the subject under discussion.

'Well, what price her playing fast and loose with me?' he cried. 'Leading me on and then starting the old army game, the two-timing Jezebel.'

'Don't you mean Delilah?'

'Do I?' said Tipton, dubious.

177

'I think so,' said Gally, none too sure himself. 'Jezebel was the one who got eaten by dogs.'

'What a beastly idea.'

'Not pleasant,' agreed Gally. 'Must have hurt like the dickens. However, the point is,' he said, a stern look coming into his face, 'that you are speaking of my niece and bringing a very serious accusation against her. What, exactly, do you imply by the expression 'the old army game'?'

'I mean she's giving me the run-around.'

'I fail to understand you.'

'Well, what would you call it if a girl let it be generally known that you were the blue-eyed boy and then you found her necking on benches with that heel Freddie?'

This shook Gally.

'Necking on benches? With Freddie?'

'I saw them. He was kissing her. She was crying, and he was kissing her like nobody's business.'

'When was this?'

'Yesterday.'

Daylight flooded in upon the Hon. Galahad. He was a man who could put two and two together.

'Before you had failed to meet her behind the rhododendrons,' he asked keenly, 'or after?'

'After,' said Tipton, and having spoken allowed his mouth to remain open like that of a sea lion expecting another fish. 'Gee! Do you think that was why she was crying?'

'Of course it was. My dear chap, you're a man of the world and you know perfectly well that you can't go about the place telling girls to meet

178

you behind rhododendrons and then not turning up without gashing their sensitive natures to the quick. One sees the whole picture. Having drawn blank in the rhododendrons, Veronica would naturally totter to the nearest bench and weep bitterly. Along comes Freddie, finds her in tears, and in a cousinly spirit kisses her.'

'Cousinly spirit? You think that was it?'

'Unquestionably. A purely cousinly spirit. They have known each other all their lives.'

'Yes,' said Tipton moodily. 'People used to call her his little sweetheart.'

'Who told you that?'

'Lord Emsworth.'

Gally clicked his tongue.

'My dear fellow, one of the first lessons you have to learn, if you intend to preserve your sanity in Blandings Castle, is to pay no attention whatsoever to anything my brother Clarence says. He has been talking through the back of his neck for nearly sixty years. I never heard anyone call Veronica Freddie's little sweetheart.'

'He used to be engaged to her.'

'Well, weren't we all? I don't mean engaged to Veronica, but to somebody. Weren't you?'

'Why, yes,' Tipton was forced to admit. 'I've been engaged about half a dozen times.'

'And they mean nothing to you now, these momentary *tendresses?*'

'Momentary what?'

'Oh, get on with it,' said Gally. 'You don't care a damn for the girls now, what?'

'I wouldn't say a damn,' said Tipton meditatively. 'There was one named Doris

179

Jimpson . . . Yes, I would too. No, I don't care a damn for any of them.'

'Exactly. Well, there you are. You needn't worry about Freddie. He's devoted to his wife.'

Hope dawned in his young friend's face.

'You mean that?'

'Certainly. A thoroughly happy marriage. They bill and coo incessantly.'

'Gosh,' said Tipton, and mused awhile. 'Of course cousins do kiss cousins, don't they?'

'They're at it all the time.'

'And it doesn't mean a thing?'

'Not a thing. Tell me, my dear chap,' said Gally, feeling that the sooner this point was settled the quicker the conference would begin to get results. 'Why did you hang back from that rhododendron tryst?'

'Well, it's a long story,' said Tipton.

It was not often that the Hon. Galahad found himself commending the shrewdness and intelligence of a nephew whom from infancy he had always looked upon as half-witted, but he did so now, as the tale of the face unfolded itself. In the course of a longish life spent in London's more Bohemian circles it had been his privilege to enjoy the friendship of quite a number of men who saw things, and he knew how sensitive and highly strung those so afflicted were, and how readily they had recourse to the bottle to ease the strain. Unquestionably, Freddie had been right. It would have been an error of the gravest nature to have put the pig in Tipton Plimsolls sleeping quarters.

'I see,' he said thoughtfully, as the narrative

180

drew to its conclusion. 'This face peered at you from the bushes?'

'Not so much peered,' said Tipton, who liked to get things straight, 'as leered. And I rather think it said 'Hi!''

'And had you given it any encouragement?'

'Well, I did take a short snort from my flask.'

'Ah! You have it here, this flask?'

'It's in that drawer over there.'

The Hon. Galahad cocked a dubious eyebrow at the drawer.

'Hadn't you better let me take charge of that?'

Tipton chewed his lip. It was as if the suggestion had been made to a drowning man that he part with his life-belt.

'It is not the sort of thing you ought to have handy. And you won't need it. Believe me, my boy, this is going to be a walkover, I know for a fact that Veronica is head over ears in love with you. No earthly need to buck yourself up before proposing.'

'The squirt thought otherwise.'

'The squirt?'

'That small, blue-eyed girl they call Prudence.'

'She advised a gargle?'

'A quick one.'

'I think she was wrong. You could do it on lime juice.'

Tipton continued dubious, but before any settlement could be reached, the debate was interrupted. From the hall below there burst upon their ears the sound of booming brass. Gally, who had been prepared for it, showed no concern, but Tipton, to whom it came as a

181

complete surprise and who for a moment had mistaken it for the Last Trump, rose an inch or two into the air.

'What the devil was that?' he asked, becoming calmer.

'Just someone fooling about,' said Gally reassuringly. 'Probably Freddie. Pay no attention. Go right up to Veronica's room and get the thing over.'

'To her room?'

'I have an idea I saw her going there.'

'But I can't muscle into a girl's room.'

'Certainly not. Just knock, and ask her to come out and speak to you. Do it now,' said the Hon. Galahad.

V

It is a truism to say that the best-laid plans are often disarranged and sometimes even defeated by the occurrence of some small unforeseen hitch in the programme. The poet Burns, it will be remembered, specifically warns the public to budget for this possibility. The gong sequence now under our notice provides a case in point.

What the Hon. Galahad had failed to allow for in arranging for Freddie to beat the gong as a signal that Veronica Wedge was on her way up to her room was that there is a certain type of girl, to which Veronica belonged, who on hearing gongs beaten when they are half-way upstairs come down again and start asking those who have beaten them why they have beaten them.

Freddie was just replacing the stick on its hook with the gratifying feeling of having completed a good bit of work when he observed a pair of enormous eyes staring into his and realized that the starter's flag had dropped prematurely.

The following dialogue took place:

'Fred-dee, was that you?'

'Was what me?'

'Did you beat the gong?'

'The gong? Oh yes. Yes, I beat the gong.'

'Why did you beat the gong?'

'Oh, I don't know. I thought I would.'

'But what did you beat the gong *for?*'

This sort of thing was threatening to go on for some time when Lady Hermione came out of the drawing-room.

Lady Hermione said:

'Who beat the gong?'

To which Veronica replied: 'Fred-die beat the gong.'

'Did you beat the gong, Freddie?'

'Er — Yes. Yes, I beat the gong.'

Lady Hermione swooped on this damaging admission like a cross-examining counsel.

'*Why* did you beat the gong?'

Veronica said that that was just what she had been asking him.

'I was going up to my room to get my album of snapshots, Mum-mee, and he suddenly beat the gong.'

Beach, the butler, appeared through the green baize door at the end of the hall.

'Did somebody beat the gong, m'lady?'

'Mr Frederick beat the gong.'

'Very good, m'lady.'

Beach withdrew, and the debate continued. It came out in the end that Freddie had beaten the gong just for a whim. A what? A *whim!* Dash it, you know how you get whims sometimes. He had got this sudden whim to beat the gong, so he had beaten the gong. He said he was blowed if he could see what all the fuss was about, and Veronica said: 'But, Fred-die,' and Lady Hermione said that America appeared to have made him even weaker in the head than he had been before crossing the Atlantic, and Veronica was just about to resume her progress up the stairs (still feeling that it was peculiar that her cousin should have beaten gongs), when it occurred to Lady Hermione that she had forgotten to tell Bellamy, her maid, to change the shoulder straps on her brassiere and that this was a task which could be very well undertaken by Veronica.

Veronica, always dutiful, said: 'Yes, Mum-mee,' and set out for the room next to the servants' hall where Bellamy did her sewing. Lady Hermione went back to the drawing-room. Freddie, feeling that the situation had got beyond him, took refuge in the billiard room, and started thinking of dog biscuits.

So that when the Hon. Galahad, misled by the beating of the gong, supposed that his niece was on her way up to her bedroom, she was really headed in a different direction altogether, and the chances of Tipton Plimsoll rescuing her from pigs and clasping her trembling form to his bosom and asking her to be his wife were for the moment nil. It was not until quite some little time later that Veronica, having delivered her message to Bellamy, turned her thoughts once more towards the fetching of snapshot albums.

Tipton, meanwhile, having reached the Red Room, had paused before its closed door. He was breathing rather stertorously, and he balanced himself first on one leg, then on the other.

In scouting Freddie's suggestion that a nephew of the late Chet Tipton might be suffering from cold feet in his relations with the opposite sex, the Hon. Galahad had erred. Nephews do not always inherit their uncles' dash and fire. You might have had to hold Chet back with ropes when there were girls around, but not Tipton. In spite of the encouragement which he had received both from Gally and the squirt Prudence, he was conscious now of a very low temperature in his extremities. Also, his heart was throbbing like a motor-cycle, and he experienced a strange difficulty in breathing. And the more he thought the situation over, the more convinced he became that a preliminary stimulant was essential to the task he had in hand.

A look of decision crept into his face. He strode from the door and hurried back to his room. The flask was still in the drawer — he shuddered to think how near he had come in a moment of weakness to yielding to Gally's offer to take charge of it — and he raised it to his lips and threw his head back.

The treatment was instantaneously effective. Resolution and courage seemed to run through

185

his veins like fire. Defiantly he looked about the room, expecting to see the face and prepared to look it in the eye and make it wilt. But no face appeared. And this final bit of good luck set the seal on his feeling of well-being.

Three minutes later he was outside the Red Room again, strong now and confident, and he lost no time in raising a hand and driving the knuckles against the panel.

It was the sort of buffet which might have been expected to produce instant results, for in his uplifted mood he had put so much follow-through into it that he had nearly broken the skin. But no voice answered from within. And this struck Tipton as odd, for there could be no question that the girl was there. He could hear her moving about. Indeed, as he paused for a reply, there came a sudden crash, suggesting that she had bumped into a table or something with china on it.

He knocked again.

'Say!' he said, putting his lips to the woodwork and speaking in a voice tense with emotion.

This time his efforts were rewarded. From the other side of the door there came an odd sound, rather like a grunt, and he took it for an invitation to enter. He had not actually expected the girl he loved to grunt, but he was not unduly surprised that she had done so. He assumed that she must have something in her mouth. Girls, he knew, often did put things in their mouths — hairpins and things like that. Doris Jimpson had frequently done this.

He turned the handle . . .

★　★　★

It was a few minutes later that Beach, the butler, passing through the baize doors into the hall on one of those errands which take butlers through baize doors into halls, was aware of a voice from above that said, 'Hey!' and, glancing up, perceived that he was being addressed by the young American gentleman whom Mr Frederick had brought to the castle.

'Sir?' said Beach.

Tipton Plimsoll's manner betrayed unmistakable agitation. His face was pale, and the eyes behind the horn-rimmed spectacles seemed heavy with some secret sorrow. His breathing would have interested an asthma specialist.

'Say, listen,' he said. 'Which is Mr Threepwood's room?'

'Mr Frederick Threepwood, sir?'

'No, the other one. The guy they call Gally.'

'Mr Galahad is occupying the Garden Suite, sir. It is on the right side of the passage which you see before you. But I fancy he is out in the grounds at the moment, sir.'

'That's all right,' said Tipton. 'I don't want to see him, just to leave something in his room. Thanks.'

He made his way with faltering footsteps to the sitting-room of the Garden Suite and, drawing the flask from his pocket, placed it on the table with something of the sad resignation of a Russian peasant regretfully throwing his infant son to a pursuing wolf pack. This done, he came slowly out and slowly started to walk upstairs once more.

And he had just reached the first landing, still in low gear, when something occurred that caused him to go abruptly into high, something that made him throw his head back like a war-horse at the sound of the bugle, square his shoulders, and skim up the stairs three at a time.

From above, seeming to proceed from the direction of the Red Room, a girl's voice had spoken, and he recognized it as that of Veronica Wedge.

'EEEEEEEEEE!!!' it was saying.

VI

A girl with good lungs cannot exclaim 'EEEEEEEEEE!!!' to the fullest extent of those lungs on the second floor of a country house during the quiet period which follows the consumption of lunch without exciting attention and interest. The afternoon being so fine, most of the residents of Blandings Castle were out in the open — Gally for one; Colonel Wedge for another; Prudence for a third; and Freddie, who had found the billiard room stuffy and had gone off to the stables to have a look at his two-seater, for a fourth. But Lady Hermione, who was in the drawing-room, got it nicely.

At the moment when the drowsy summer stillness was ripped into a million quivering fragments, Lady Hermione had been reading for the third time a telegram which had just been brought to her on a silver salver by Beach, the butler. Signed 'Clarence' and despatched from Paddington Station at 12.40, it ran as follows:

ARRIVING TEA TIME WITH LANDLADY

When Lord Emsworth composed telegrams in railway stations two minutes before his train was due to leave, his handwriting, never at the best of times copperplate, always degenerated into something which would have interested a Professor of Hieroglyphics. The operator at Paddington, after a puzzled scrutiny, had substituted on his own responsibility 'Arriving' for 'Ariosto' and 'teatime' for what appeared to be 'totem' but the concluding word had beaten him completely. It had seemed to him a choice between 'lingfear', 'leprosy', and 'landlady'. He had discarded the first because there is no such word as 'lingfear'; the second because, though not a medical expert, he was pretty sure that Lord Emsworth had not got leprosy; and had fallen back on the third. He hoped that it would convey some meaning at the other end.

He had been too optimistic. Lady Hermione stared at the missive blankly. Its surface import — that the head of the family, when he showed up for the afternoon cup of tea, would be accompanied by something stout in a sealskin coat and a Sunday bonnet — she rejected. If it had been her brother Galahad who had so telegraphed, it would have been another matter. Galahad, being the sort of man he was, might quite conceivably have decided to present himself at Blandings Castle with a landlady, or

189

even a bevy of landladies, explaining that they had been dear friends of his years ago when they used to do clog dances on the halls. But not Clarence. She had never been blind to the fact that the head of the family was eccentric, but she knew him to be averse from feminine society. Landladies who wanted a breath of country air would never get it on his invitation.

She was just wondering if the word could possibly be a misprint for 'laryngitis', a malady from which the ninth earl occasionally suffered, when Veronica went on the air.

To refresh the reader's memory, in case he has forgotten, what Veronica was saying was 'EEEEEEEEEEEE!!!' and as soon as she had made certain that the top of her head had not come off Lady Hermione found the cry speaking to her very depths. A moment's startled rigidity and she was racing up the stairs at a speed not much inferior to that recently shown by Tipton. It is a callous mother who can remain in a drawing-room when her child is squealing 'EEEEEEEEEEE!!!' on the second floor.

Her pace was still good as she rounded into the straight, but as she came in sight of the door of the Red Room she braked sharply. There had met her eyes a spectacle so arresting, so entrancing, so calculated to uplift a mother's heart and make her want to turn cartwheels along the corridor that she feared for an instant that it might be a mirage. Blinking and looking again, she saw that she had not been deceived.

There, half-way down the corridor, one of the richest young men in America was clasping her daughter to his chest, and even as she gazed he bestowed upon that daughter a kiss so ardent that there could be no mistaking its meaning.

'Veronica!' she cried. A lesser woman would have said 'Whoopee!'

Tipton, tensely occupied, had been unaware till now that he was not alone with his future wife. Turning to include his future mother-in-law in the conversation, his immediate impulse, for he was an American gentleman, was to make it clear to her that this was the real stuff and not one of those licentious scenes which Philadelphia censors cut out of pictures.

'It's quite O.K.,' he hastened to assure her. 'We're engaged.'

Her dash up the stairs had left Lady Hermione a little touched in the wind, and for a space she remained panting. Eventually she was able to say: 'Oh, Tipton!'

'You are not losing a daughter,' said Tipton, having had time to think of a good one. 'You are gaining a son.'

Any doubts which he might have entertained as to the popularity of his romance in the circles most immediately interested were at once removed. It was abundantly clear that the arrangement which he had outlined was one that had Lady Hermione's sympathy and support. Her breath now recovered, she kissed him with a warmth that left no room for misunderstanding.

'Oh, Tipton!' she said again. 'I am delighted. You must be very happy, Veronica.'

'Yes, Mum-mee.'

'Such a lovely birthday present for you,

darling,' said Lady Hermione.

Her words got right in amongst Tipton Plimsoll. He started as if a whole platoon of faces had suddenly manifested themselves before his eyes. He remembered now that at breakfast somebody had been saying something about it being somebody's birthday, but he had been moody and abstracted and had not thought to enquire into the matter. A vague impression had been left upon his mind that they had been talking about the squirt Prudence.

Remorse shot through him like a red-hot skewer. It seemed incredible to him that preoccupation should have caused him to remain in ignorance of this vital fact.

'Jiminy Christmas!' he cried, aghast. 'Is this your birthday? And I haven't got you a present. I must get you a present. Where can I get you a present?'

'Shrewsbury,' said Veronica. She was at her best when answering simple, straightforward questions like that.

Tipton's air was now that of one straining at the leash.

'How long does it take you to get to Shrewsbury?'

'About three quarters of an hour in a car.'

'Are there shops there?'

'Oh, yes.'

'Jewellers' shops?'

'Oh *yes!*'

'Then meet me in the rhododendrons in about a couple of hours and anticipate a pleasant surprise. I'll go swipe a car. Oh, say,' said Tipton, recollecting something which, though of minor importance compared with birthday presents for the girl he loved, deserved, he felt, a passing mention. 'There's a pig in there.'

'A pig?'

'Yes, Mum-mee, there's a pig in my bedroom.'

'Most extraordinary,' said Lady Hermione, and might have been sceptical had not the Empress selected this moment for thrusting a mild and enquiring face round the door.

'There you are,' said Tipton. 'One pig, as stated.'

He left her to cope with it. He felt that the matter could be in no better hands. On flying feet he hastened to the stables.

Freddie was in the yard, tinkering with his two-seater.

VII

There had been a time, and that not so long ago, when, finding Freddie in stable yards tinkering with two-seaters, Tipton Plimsoll would have drawn himself to his full height and passed by with a cold stare. But now that he had wooed and won the most beautiful girl in the world he was in softer, kindlier mood. He had erased the other's name from his list of snakes and saw him for what he was — a blameless cousin.

Later on, no doubt, they would have to come to some arrangement about the other's habit of bestowing cousinly kisses on the future Mrs Plimsoll, but for the moment there was no jarring note to cause a discord between them. Filled to the brim with the milk of human kindness, Tipton regarded Freddie once more as a pal and a buddy. And when you are sitting on top of the world, the first people you apprise of the fact are pals and buddies. He lost no time in announcing the great news.

'Say, Freddie,' he said, 'guess what? I'm engaged!'

'Engaged?'

'Yup.'

'To Vee?'

'Sure. Just signed on the dotted line.'

'Well, I'm dashed,' said Freddie. 'Put it there, pardner.'

So beaming was his smile, so cordial his handshake, that Tipton found his last doubts removed. And so beaming was *his* smile, so instinct with benevolence his whole demeanour, that Freddie decided that the moment had arrived to put his fate to the test, to win or lose it all.

This necessitated a somewhat abrupt change of subject, but he was feeling too tense to lead the conversation around to the thing in easy stages.

'Oh, by the way, old man,' he said.

'Yes, old man?' said Tipton.

'There's something I've been meaning to ask you for some time, old man,' said Freddie, 'only it kept slipping my mind. Will you give the Tipton's Stores dog biscuit concession to Donaldson's Dog-Joy, old man?'

'Why, sure, old man,' said Tipton, looking like

something out of Dickens. 'I was going to suggest it myself.'

The stable yard seemed to reel before Freddie's eyes. He stood silent for an instant, struggling with his emotion. In his mind he was sketching out the cable which he would despatch that night to Long Island City, informing his father-in-law of this outstanding triumph which he had achieved in the interests of the dog biscuits he loved so well. He could picture the old buster opening the envelope and going into a hootchy-kootchy dance all over the office.

He drew a long breath.

'Old man,' he said reverently, 'they don't come any whiter than you. I've always said so.'

'Have you, old man?'

'I certainly have. And I hope you'll be very, very happy, old man.'

'Thanks, old man. Say, can I borrow your car? I want to go to Shrewsbury and buy Veronica a birthday present.'

'I'll drive you there, old man.'

'That's darned good of you, old man.'

'Not at all, old man, not at all,' said Freddie.

He seated himself at the wheel and placed a suede-clad shoe on the self-starter. It occurred to him as a passing thought that all was for the best in this best of all possible worlds.

8

I

A man who likes to see the young folks happy always finds it agreeable to be able to reflect that owing to his ministrations joy among the younger set is reigning unconfined; and the events of the summer afternoon had left the Hon. Galahad Threepwood feeling at the peak of his form.

He had just met his niece Veronica on her way to the rhododendrons and had been informed by her of the signal good fortune which had befallen the house of Wedge. And before that he had come upon his niece Prudence palely loitering in the drive and had given her Bill's letter, thereby bringing the roses back to her cheeks and causing her to revise her views on the sadness of life from the bottom up. As he came out of the sunshine into the dim coolness of the hall he was walking jauntily and humming beneath his breath a gay music-hall ballad of his youth.

It was now the hour when the fragrance of tea and the warm, heartening scent of buttered toast begin to float like a benediction over the English home, and Beach and his capable assistants had already set out the makings in the drawing-room. He proceeded to trip thither, but more from sociability than with any idea of becoming an active participant in the feast. He never drank tea, having always had a prejudice against the stuff since his friend Buffy Struggles back in the nineties had taken to it as a substitute for alcohol and had perished miserably as a result. (Actually what had led to the late Mr Struggles's turning in his dinner pail had been a collision in Piccadilly with a hansom cab, but Gally had always felt that this could have been avoided if the poor dear old chap had not undermined his constitution by swilling a beverage whose dangers are recognized by every competent medical authority.)

The drawing-room was empty except for his sister Hermione, who was seated behind the teapot, ready to get into action the instant the call came. She stiffened as he entered and directed at him a stern and accusing glare, like a well-bred basilisk.

'So there you are, Galahad,' she said, coming to the point in the direct way characteristic of sisters all the world over. Galahad, what do you mean by putting that beastly pig in Veronica's bedroom?'

This was not clairvoyance. Lady Hermione had reached her conclusion by a careful process of character analysis. Probing into the natures and dispositions of her little circle, she had decided that there was only one person on the premises capable of putting pigs in bedrooms and that that person stood before her now.

The arrival of Beach at this moment with a bowl of strawberries, followed by a footman bearing cream and another staggering under the weight of powdered sugar, prevented an immediate reply to the question. When the procession had filed out, Beach in transit booking an order for a whisky and soda, Gally was able to speak.

'So you've heard about that?' he said airily.

'Heard about it? The loathsome animal was galloping all over the corridor.'

'It was a clever idea,' said Gally, with modest pride. 'Yes, though I say it myself, clever. Egbert was weeping on my shoulder this morning about the way young Plimsoll was shillyshallying. I saw that it was no time for half-measures. I acted. To whisk the Empress from her sty and put her in the forefront of the battle was with me the work of an instant. Did Veronica yowl?'

'She screamed,' corrected his sister coldly. 'The poor child received a very severe shock.'

'And Plimsoll, I gather, dashed up and came to the rescue. The ice was broken. He lost his reserve. He folded her in his arms and spoke his love, and a wedding has been arranged and will shortly take place. Just as I foresaw. Precisely as I had anticipated. The whole operation from start to finish went according to plan, and the curtain fell on the happy ending. So what you're blinding and stiffing about,' said Gally, who, unlike Lord Emsworth, was not the man to be browbeaten by sisters, 'I fail to understand.'

Lady Hermione denied the charge that she was blinding and stiffing. She was, she said, extremely annoyed.

'Annoyed? What the dickens is there to be annoyed about?'

'The animal ate one of Veronica's new camisoles.'

'Well, finding itself in the bedroom, it would naturally assume that it had been invited to take pot luck. Stick to the point, which is that you can't get away from it that, but for my subtle strategy, business would never have resulted. Dash it, which would the girl rather have — a mouldy camisole or a wealthy and devoted husband whose only thought will be to gratify her lightest wish? Young Plimsoll will be able to provide Veronica with diamond camisoles, if she wants them. So stop cursing and swearing like a bargee, and let's see that sunny smile of yours. Can't you realize that this is the maddest, merriest day of all the glad New Year?'

The soundness of his reasoning was so manifest that Lady Hermione was obliged to relax her austerity. She did not actually smile her sunny smile, but a trace of softness crept into her demeanour, which up till now had resembled that of a rather unusually stern governess.

'Well, I have no doubt that your motives were excellent, but I hope you will not do it again.'

'You don't suppose a busy man like me makes a practice of putting pigs in girls' rooms? What became of the animal in the final issue?'

'The pig man removed it.'

'I must remember to fling him a purse of gold, or he'll go squealing to Clarence. What would you say was the market price of a pig man's silence? How did you get in touch with him?'

'I rang for Beach, who sent a footman to fetch him. A little gnome of a man with no roof to his mouth who smelled worse than the pig.'

'Niffy, eh? It probably covered an honest heart. Niffiness often does. And we can't all have roofs to our mouths. When are you expecting Clarence back?'

'He wired that he would be here for tea.'

'Odd how he enjoys his cup of tea. Can't think why. Horrible muck. Polished off poor old Buffy Struggles as clean as a whistle.'

'Here's his telegram. It arrived just before Veronica received that terrible shock.'

In Gally's opinion this remark came under the heading of harping on the dead past.

'I wish you wouldn't keep burbling on about Veronica receiving shocks,' he said impatiently. 'You talk as if finding a simple pig in her room were enough to disintegrate her entire nervous system. I don't suppose that after her first natural surprise she experienced any discomfort whatsoever. What did Clarence say in his telegram?'

'That he would be arriving at tea time with landlady.'

'With what?'

'Read it for yourself.'

Gally fixed his black-rimmed monocle more firmly in his eye and scrutinized the document. His face cleared.

'I can tell you what this means. What he was trying to say in that vile handwriting of his was that he would be accompanied by Landseer.'

'Landseer?'

'The artist.'

'Landseer is dead.'

'He wasn't when I met him yesterday.'

'Do you mean the Landseer who painted stags?'

'No. I mean the Landseer who paints pigs.'

'I never heard of him.'

'Well, cheer up. You're hearing of him now. And you'll be meeting him in a few minutes. Clarence has commissioned him on my recommendation to do the Empress's portrait.'

Lady Hermione uttered a sharp cry.

'You have not been encouraging Clarence in that idiotic idea of his?'

'He didn't need any encouraging. He came up to London full of iron resolution, determined to procure an artist of some kind. All I did was to assist him in his choice. You'll like this fellow. Charming chap.'

'A friend of yours?'

'Yes,' replied Gally, with spirit. 'A very dear friend of mine. What did you say?'

Lady Hermione said that she had not spoken. Nor had she. She had merely sniffed. But in certain circumstances a sniff can be as wounding as the bitterest repartee, and Gally was about to comment on hers in a militant manner, for his lifelong policy had been to be very firm with sniffing sisters, when there came the sound of wheels grinding to a standstill on the gravel outside the front door.

'Clarence,' said Gally.

'And Mr Landseer.'

'Don't say 'And Mr Landseer' in that soupy tone of voice,' said Gally sternly 'He hasn't come to steal the spoons.'

'If he is a friend of yours, I should imagine that he is quite capable of doing so. Is he wanted by the police?'

'No, he is not wanted by the police.'

'How I sympathize with the police,' said Lady Hermione. 'I know just how they feel.'

From the hall the reedy tenor voice of Lord Emsworth cut in upon a conversation which was threatening to become acrimonious.

'Beach will show you your room, my dear fellow,' he was saying, addressing an unseen companion. 'Tell you where it is and so forth. Come along to the drawing-room when you're ready.'

And presently the seigneur of Blandings Castle entered, inhaling the grateful odour that rose from the teapot and beaming vaguely through his pince-nez.

'Ah,' he said. 'Tea, eh? Tea. Capital, capital. Tea.' Then, following his custom of making his meaning thoroughly clear, added the word 'Tea,' repeating it three times. The dullest listener would have divined that he was aware of the presence of tea and would be glad of a cup, and Lady Hermione, pausing only to sniff, poured him out one.

'Tea,' said Lord Emsworth again, clearing the whole situation up and getting everything straight. 'Thank you, my dear.' He took the cup, cleverly added milk and sugar, stirred, and drank. 'Ha!' he ejaculated, refreshed. 'Well, here I am, Galahad.'

'You never spoke a truer word, Clarence,' his brother agreed. 'I can see you with the naked eye. Did you bring Landseer?'

'Who is Landseer? Oh, of course, yes, Landseer. I was forgetting. That was Landseer I was talking to in the hall. Landseer,' explained Lord Emsworth, addressing his sister, 'is an artist who has come to paint the Empress.'

'So Galahad was telling me,' said Lady Hermione.

Her tone was so free from joyous animation that Gally felt constrained to supply a footnote.

'Hermione is anti-Landseer. She has taken one of her absurd prejudices against the poor chap.'

'I have done nothing of the kind,' said Lady Hermione. 'I preserve an open mind on the subject of Mr Landseer. I am quite prepared to find him reasonably respectable, even though he is a friend of yours. I merely feel, as I have always felt, that it is a ridiculous waste of money to have that pig's portrait painted.'

Lord Emsworth stiffened. He was shocked, not only by the sentiment but by the allusion to his ewe lamb as 'that pig'. He felt it to be lacking in respect.

'The Empress has twice in successive years won the silver medal in the Fat Pigs class at the Shrewsbury Show,' he reminded her coldly.

'Exactly,' said Gally. 'The only celebrity we have ever produced. She has a far better right to be in the family portrait gallery than half those bearded bounders who disfigure it.'

Lady Hermione became rigid. Like her sisters, she revered her ancestors with an almost Chinese fervour and had always resented the casual attitude towards them of the male members of the family.

'Well, we will not discuss it,' she said, closing the debate. 'I hope you remembered to buy Veronica her birthday present, Clarence?'

From sheer force of habit Lord Emsworth started guiltily. And he was just about to assume the weak, blustering manner customary with him on these occasions and to demand how the dickens a man like himself, with a hundred calls on his time, could be expected to remember to buy birthday presents, when he recollected that he had done so.

'Certainly I did,' he replied with dignity. 'A most excellent wrist watch. I have it in my pocket.'

He produced it as he spoke with quiet pride, and with it another package also bearing the famous label of the Bond Street firm of Aspinall, at which he peered perplexedly.

'Now what the deuce is this?' he queried. 'Ah, yes, I remember. It is something Freddie asked me to pick up at the shop. His present for Veronica, I understand. Where is Freddie?' he asked, scanning the furniture vaguely as if expecting to see his younger son lurking behind some chair or settee.

'I saw him going hell for leather down the drive in that car of his about two hours ago,' said Gally. 'He had young Plimsoll with him. I don't know where they were off to.'

'Shrewsbury,' said Lady Hermione. 'Tipton wanted to buy Veronica a birthday present. They are engaged, Clarence.'

'Eh?'

'They are engaged.'

'Ah,' said Lord Emsworth, becoming interested in a plate of cucumber sandwiches. 'Sandwiches, eh? Sandwiches, sandwiches. Sandwiches,' he added, taking one.

'They are engaged,' said Lady Hermione, raising her voice.

'Who?'

'Veronica and dear Tipton.'

'Who is dear Tipton?'

'"Dear Tipton,"' explained Gally, 'is Hermione's nickname for young Plimsoll.'

'Plimsoll? Plimsoll? Plimsoll? Oh, *Plimsoll'7d* I remember him,' said Lord Emsworth, pleased at his quick intelligence. 'You mean the young man with those extraordinary spectacles. What about him?'

'I am trying to tell you,' said Lady Hermione patiently, 'that he and Veronica are engaged.'

'God bless my soul!' said Lord Emsworth, a look of startled concern coming into his face. 'I didn't know these sandwiches were cucumber. I thought they were potted meat. I would never have eaten one if I'd known they were cucumber.'

'Oh, Clarence!'

'Can't digest cucumber. Never could.'

'Well, really, Clarence. I thought you might take a little interest in your niece.'

'What's she been doing?'

'They keep these things from you, Clarence,' said Gally sympathetically. 'You ought to be told. Veronica and young Plimsoll are engaged.'

'Ah,' said Lord Emsworth, now thoroughly

abreast of the position of affairs. 'Well, that's all right. No harm in that. I like him. He is sound on pigs.'

'And Hermione likes him because he's a millionaire,' said Gally. 'So you're all happy.'

Lady Hermione was asserting with some warmth that her fondness for Tipton Plimsoll was due entirely to the fact that he was a charming, cultured young man and devoted to Veronica, and Gally was challenging her to deny that at least a portion of the Plimsoll glamour proceeded from the circumstance of his having got the stuff in sackfuls, and Lord Emsworth was saying again that he would never have eaten that cucumber sandwich if he had known it was cucumber, because cucumbers did something to his inside, when Freddie appeared in the French windows.

'Hullo, Guv'nor. Hullo, Aunt Hermione. Hullo, Uncle Gally,' said Freddie. 'Hope I'm not too late for a beaker. We rather overstayed our time in Shrewsbury owing to Tippy insisting on buying up the whole place. The two-seater returned laden with apes, ivory, and peacocks like a camel of the epoch of King Solomon. Did you remember to pick up that little thing of mine at Aspinall's, Guv'nor?'

Secure in the fact that he was holding it in his hand, Lord Emsworth permitted himself to become testy.

'Certainly I did. Everybody asks me if I have remembered something. I never forget anything. Here it is.'

'Thanks, Guv'nor. A quick cup of tea, and I'll

go and give it to her.'

'Where is Veronica?' asked Lady Hermione.

'Tippy was expecting to locate her in the rhododendrons. They had a date there, I understand.'

'Go and tell them to come in to tea. Poor Tipton must be exhausted after his long drive.'

'He didn't seem to be. He was panting emotionally and breathing flame through the nostrils. God bless my soul,' said Freddie, 'how it brings back one's bachelor days, does it not, to think of young lovers hobnobbing in shrubberies. I often used to foregather with Aggie in the local undergrowth in my courting days, I recollect. Well, I will do my best to get your kindly message through to him, Aunt Hermione, but always with the proviso that I am not muscling in on a sacred moment. If in my judgement he doesn't want to be interrupted, I shall tiptoe away and leave him. See you later, folks. Pip-pip, Guv'nor; don't take any wooden nickels.'

He drained his cup and departed, and Lord Emsworth had just begun to say that since his younger son had returned from America he had observed in him a sort of horrible briskness and jumpiness which he deplored, when there came from without the sound of some heavy body tripping over a rug, and Bill came in.

II

Bill was looking fresher than might have been expected after a four-hour railway journey with

207

Lord Emsworth, the explanation of this being that the latter always slept in the train, so that he had had nothing to do but lie back and look out of the window and think long thoughts of Prudence.

These had been not only loving, but optimistic. Well in advance of his arrival, he presumed, Gally would have given her that letter of his, and from its perusal he confidently expected the happiest results. He had put his whole heart into the communication, and when a man with a heart as large as his does that, something has got to give. The Prue whom he would shortly meet would, he anticipated, be a vastly different Prue from the scornful girl who had called him a fathead, broken the engagement, and whizzed off like a jack rabbit before he could even start to appeal to her better nature.

But though such reflections as these had unquestionably tended to raise his spirits, it would be too much to say that William Lister, as he clumped across the threshold of the drawing-room of Blandings Castle, was feeling completely carefree. He was in the pink, yes, but not so entirely in the pink as to preclude a certain wariness and anxiety. His mental attitude might be compared to that of a cat entering a strange alley whose resident population may or may not be possessed of half-bricks and inspired with the urge to heave them.

To the discomfort of being in the society of an elderly gentleman whom in a moment of pique he had once told to go and boil his head he had become inured. He no longer regarded Lord

Emsworth as a potential obstacle in his path. The occasional puzzled stares which the other had bestowed upon him in the train before stretching out his legs and closing his eyes and starting to grunt and gurgle had fallen off him like blunted arrows. That the thought behind these stares was that Lord Emsworth was conscious of a nebulous feeling that his face was somehow familiar, he was aware; but basing his trust on the statement of the Hon. Galahad that the ninth earl had an I.Q. thirty points lower than a jellyfish he had been enabled to meet with an easy nonchalance the pince-nezed eyes that gazed perplexedly into his.

But the formidable woman seated behind the teapot was a different proposition. Here, beyond a question, danger lurked. You might not admire Lady Hermione Wedge as you would admire Helen of Troy, or the current Miss America, but there was no gainsaying her intelligence. It would have to be an exceptionally up-and-coming jellyfish which could even contemplate challenging her I.Q. He could only hope that at their previous encounter the beard had done its silent work well, obscuring his features beyond recognition.

Her greeting, if you could call it a greeting, seemed to suggest that everything was all right so far. She was unable entirely to conceal the fact that she regarded him as a pest and an intruder who if she had had her way would have been dumped at the Emsworth Arms and not allowed to inflict his beastly presence on a decent castle; but she directed at him no quick, suspicious stare, uttered no sharp cry of denunciation. She said: 'How do you do, Mr Landseer,' in a voice that suggested that she hoped he was going to tell her that the doctors had given him three weeks to live, and supplied him with a cup of tea. Bill knocked over a cake table, and they all settled down to make a cosy evening of it.

Conversation became general. Lord Emsworth, sniffing the scented breeze which floated in through the open windows, said that it was nice to be back in civilized surroundings after a visit to London, and Gally said that he had never been able to understand his brother's objections to London, a city which he himself had always found an earthly Paradise. He applied to Bill to support him in this view, and Bill, who had fallen into a dream about Prudence, started convulsively and kicked over the small table on which he had placed his cup. In response to his apologies Lady Hermione assured him that it did not matter in the least. Anybody who had not caught her eye, as Bill did, would have supposed her to be one of those broad-minded hostesses who prefer tea on their carpets.

Lord Emsworth then said that his distaste for London was due to the circumstance of it being a nasty, noisy, filthy, smelly hole, full of the most frightful cads, and Gally said that they were probably all charming chaps once you got to know them, instancing the case of a one-eyed three-card-trick man back in the early days of the century to whom he had taken an unreasoning dislike at their first meeting, only to discover, after they had been on a binge together one evening, that the fellow was the salt of the earth.

Lady Hermione, who deprecated the introduction into the tea-table conversation in her drawing-room of reminiscences of one-eyed three-card-trick men, however sound their hearts, changed the subject by asking Bill if this was his first visit to Shropshire, and the latter, shaken to his foundations by the innocent query, once more kicked over the cake table. The fact was that Bill, though an admirable character, was always a little large for any room in which he was confined. To ensure his not kicking over cake tables, you would have had to place him in the Gobi Desert.

Gally in his genial way had just offered, if Bill wanted to make a nice clean job of smashing up the premises, to bring him an axe, and was asking Lord Emsworth if he remembered the time when their mutual uncle, Harold, who had never been quite himself after that touch of sunstroke in the East, had wrecked this same drawing-room with a borrowed meatchopper in an attempt to kill a wasp, when Lady Hermione, who had been regarding Bill with quiet loathing, suddenly gave a start and intensified her scrutiny.

It had just occurred to her, as it had occurred to Lord Emsworth in Duke Street, that somewhere, at some time and place, she had seen him before.

'Your face seems oddly familiar, Mr Landseer,' she said, gazing at it with a raptness which only

211

Tipton Plimsoll could have surpassed.

Lord Emsworth peered through his pince-nez, intrigued.

'Just what I said when I met him. Struck me at once. It's a peculiar face,' he said, scanning it closely and noting that it had now turned a rich vermilion. 'Sort of face that stamps itself on the memory. Galahad's suggestion was that I must have seen his photograph in the papers.'

'Does Mr Landseer's photograph appear in the papers?' asked Lady Hermione, her tone suggesting that, if so, it lowered her opinion of the British Press.

'Of course it does,' said Gally, correctly divining that Bill would appreciate a helping hand. 'Repeatedly. As I told Clarence, Landseer is a dashed celebrated chap.'

Lord Emsworth endorsed this view.

'He painted the Stag at Bay,' he said admiringly.

There was a special sound which Lady Hermione often found it convenient to employ when conversing with her elder brother and feeling the need of relieving her feelings. It was not exactly a sniff and not precisely a snort, but a sort of blend of the two. It proceeded from her now.

'Mr Landseer did not paint the Stag at Bay. It was painted by Sir Edwin Landseer, who has been dead for years.'

'That's odd. Galahad told me it was this chap who painted the Stag at Bay'

Gally laughed indulgently.

'You've muddled the whole thing as usual,

Clarence. I said the Pig at Bay'

'The *Pig* at Bay?'

'Yes. A very different thing.'

Lord Emsworth digested this. A question occurred to him almost immediately.

'But are pigs at bay?'

'This one was.'

'It seems most unusual.'

'Not when you remember, as you would if you were a travelled man, that Bée is a village in the Pyrenees famous for its pigs. If Landseer goes to Bée on a sketching tour one summer and sees a pig there and paints it and, hunting round for a title, decides to call it the Pig at Bée, it seems to me quite a natural sequence of events. I don't see what all the argument is about, anyway. The only thing that matters, to my mind, is that you have got hold of a man who knows his pigs and can be relied on to turn out a speaking likeness of the Empress. You ought to be rejoicing unstintedly.'

'Oh, I am,' said Lord Emsworth. 'Oh, yes, indeed. It's a great relief to feel that Mr Landseer is going to attend to the thing. I'm sure he will be an enormous improvement on the other fellow. By George!' cried Lord Emsworth with sudden animation. 'God bless my soul! Now I know why I thought I'd seen him before. He's the living image of that other fellow — the frightful chap you sent down a few days ago, the one who did a horrible caricature of the Empress and then told me to go and boil my head because I ventured on the mildest of criticisms. What was his name?'

'Messmore Breamworthy.' Gally eyed Bill with mild interest. 'Yes, there is a resemblance,' he agreed. 'Quite understandably of course, considering that they are half-brothers.'

'Eh?'

'Landseer's widowed mother married a man named Bream-worthy. The union culminated in young Messmore. A good enough chap in his way, but I would never have sent him down if I had known that Landseer was available. No comparison between the two men as artists.'

'Odd that they should both be artists.'

'Would you say that? Surely these things often run in families.'

'That's true,' agreed Lord Emsworth. 'There's a man living near here who breeds cocker spaniels, and he has a brother in Kent who breeds sealyhams.'

During these exchanges Lady Hermione had been silent. It was the burgeoning within her of a monstrous suspicion that had made her so. Slowly and by degrees this suspicion was gathering strength. Indeed, the only barrier to a complete understanding on her part was the feeling that there must surely be some things of which her brother Galahad was not capable. She knew him to be a man possessed to an impressive degree of the gall of an army mule, but even an army mule, she considered, would hesitate to smuggle into Blandings Castle an ineligible suitor from whose society one of its sacred nieces was being rigorously withheld.

She looked at Bill and closed her eyes, trying to conjure up that interview on the lawn. She wished she could be sure . . .

Too little, the chronicler realizes, has been said about that beard of Fruity Biffen's, and it may be that its concealing properties have not been adequately stressed. But reading between the lines, the public must have gathered an impression of its density. The Fruities of this world, when they are endeavouring to baffle the scrutiny of keen-eyed bookmakers, do not skimp in the matter of face fungus. The man behind this beard was not so much a man wearing a beard as a pair of eyes staring out of an impenetrable jungle; and, try as she might, Lady Hermione was unable to recall any more definite picture than just that.

She sat back in her chair frowning. The whole thing turned, of course, on whether her brother Galahad was or was not capable of drawing the line somewhere. She mused on this, and the conversation flowed about her unheard.

As a matter of fact, there was nothing in it particularly worth hearing. Lord Emsworth said that he had been wrong in asserting that the man who lived near here bred cocker spaniels — he had meant retrievers. And as the mention of dogs of any breed could scarcely fail to remind Gally of a rather amusing story which might possibly be new to those present, he told one.

He had finished it and was starting another, begging them to stop him if they had heard it before, when Lord Emsworth, who had been showing signs of restlessness, said that he thought he ought to be going down and seeing Pott, his pig man, in case the latter should have

215

anything of interest to report concerning the affairs of the Empress during his absence.

The words brought Gally to an abrupt halt in his narrative. They reminded him that he had still to see this Pott and purchase his silence. If Lord Emsworth were to contact the fellow before this was done, who knew what sensational confidences might not be poured into his quivering ear. Gally was extremely fond of his brother and shrank from having him upset. He also disliked arguments and discussions.

Policy plainly called to him to race off and sweeten Pott. But this involved leaving Bill. And was it safe to leave Bill to cope unsupported with a situation which he was quite aware was delicate and difficult?

The point was very moot, and for a moment he hesitated. What finally decided him was Lady Hermione's trancelike demeanour. She seemed to have withdrawn into a meditative coma, and as long as this persisted there could surely be no peril. And, after all, it does not take the whole evening to whizz down to a pigsty, stop the pig man's mouth with gold, and whizz back again. He would be able to return in a quarter of an hour at the outside.

Rising, accordingly, with a muttered statement about having forgotten something, he passed through the French windows and disappeared; and a few moments later Lord Emsworth, who always took a little time to collect his hands and feet when about to potter from any given spot, followed him. With much the same unpleasant shock which must have come to the boy who stood on the burning deck, Bill awoke from a reverie on his favourite subject of Prudence to the realization that all but he had fled and that he was alone with his hostess.

A silence ensued. When a young man of shy disposition, accustomed to the more Bohemian society of Chelsea, finds himself alone on her home ground with a daughter of a hundred earls and cannot forget that at their last meeting he mistook her for the cook and tipped her half a crown; and when the daughter of the hundred earls, already strongly prejudiced against the young man as an intruder, has begun to suspect that he is the miscreant who recently chivvied her only child and is doing his best to marry her niece against the wishes of the family, it is almost too much to expect that the conversation will proceed from the first with an easy flow.

Her friends had sometimes said of Lady Hermione, who was a well-read, well-educated woman with an interest in most of the problems of the day, that if she wanted to she could found a modern *salon*. At the moment, it seemed, she did not want to, at any rate with Bill as the nucleus of it.

The two were still eyeing each other with embarrassment on the one side and an ever-increasing suspicion on the other, when their *tête-à-tête* was interrupted. A shadow fell on the pool of sunlight in the French windows, and Freddie came curvetting in.

'No dice,' announced Freddie, addressing his aunt. 'I found them linked in a close embrace, and I hadn't the heart to interrupt them.'

At this point he observed that his father and his uncle were no longer in the room, but that a newcomer had been added in the shape of a large individual who was sitting with his long legs twined round those of a chair. Coming out of the sunshine, he experienced a momentary difficulty in seeing this substantial bird steadily and seeing him whole, and for an instant supposed himself to be gazing upon a stranger. The thought occurred to him that it might be possible to interest the man in a good dog biscuit.

Then, as his eyes adjusted themselves to the subdued light, they suddenly widened in an incredulous stare and his mouth, as was its habit in times of emotion, fell open like a letter box.

To his Uncle Galahad he later put two simple questions, explaining that on these he rested his case.

They were:

(a) How the dickens could he have been expected to know? and, arising from this,

(b) Why had he not been kept informed?

It stands to reason, argued Freddie, that if a chap has been widely publicized as a pariah and an outcast and then you suddenly come upon him sitting at his ease in the drawing-room, having a cosy dish of tea with the spearhead of the opposition, you naturally assume that the red light has turned to green and that he has been taken to the family's bosom. Particularly, he added with quiet reproach, if you have been expressly told that he is 'all right' and that you need not worry about him because the speaker

218

assures you that he has his case 'well in hand'.

It was on those phrases, he said, that he took his stand. Had his Uncle Gally used them, or had he not? Had he or had he not practically stated in so many words that the ban on poor old Blister had been lifted and that his future need cause his friends and well-wishers no concern? Very well, then, there you were. The point he was making was that it was unjust and absurd to apply such a term as 'cloth-headed young imbecile' to himself and to hurl at him the reproach of being a spiller of beans and a bunger of spanners into works.

What had brought about the disaster, he urged, was the Hon. Galahad's extraordinary policy of silence and secretiveness. A word to the effect that he was planning to introduce Bill Lister into the house surreptitiously, and all would have been well. In these affairs, he pointed out, co-operation is of the essence. Without co-operation and a frank pooling of information, no dividends can be expected to result.

Thus Freddie later. What he said now was:

'Blister!'

The word rang through the drawing-room like a bugle, and Lady Hermione, on whose heart the name 'Lister' was deeply graven, leaped in her chair.

'Well, well, well!' said Freddie, beaming profusely. 'Well, well, well, well, well! Well, this is fine, this is splendid. So you've seen reason, Aunt Hermione? I was hoping your sterling good sense would assert itself. I take it that you have talked Aunt Dora over, or propose to do so at an early date. Now that you are wholeheartedly on the side of love's young dream, I anticipate no trouble in that quarter. She will be wax in your hands. Tell her from me, in case she starts beefing, that Prue could find no worthier mate than good old Bill Lister. One of the best and brightest. I've known him for years. And if he chucks his art, as he has guaranteed to do, and goes into the pub-keeping business, I see no reason why the financial future of the young couple should not be extremely bright. There's money in pubs. They will need a spot of capital, of course, but that can be supplied. I suggest a family round-table conference, at which the thing can be thoroughly gone into and threshed out in all its aspects. Cheerio, Blister. Heartiest congratulations.'

Throughout this well-phased harangue Lady Hermione had been sitting with twitching hands and gleaming eyes. It had not occurred to the speaker that there was anything ominous in her demeanour, but a more observant nephew would have noted her strong resemblance to the puma of the Indian jungle about to pounce upon its prey.

She eyed him enquiringly.

'Have you quite finished, Freddie?'

'Eh? Yes, I think that about covers the subject.'

'Then I should be glad,' said Lady Hermione, 'if you would go and see Beach and tell him to pack Mr Lister's things, if they are already unpacked, and send them to the Emsworth Arms. Mr Lister will be leaving the castle immediately.'

9

I

Accustomed from earliest years to carry out with promptness and civility the wishes of his aunts, a nephew's automatic reaction to a command from one of the platoon, even after he has become a solid married man with an important executive post in America's leading firm of dog biscuit manufacturers, is to jump to it. Ordered by his Aunt Hermione to go and see Beach, Freddie did not draw himself up and reply that if she desired to get in touch with her staff she could jolly well ring for them; he started off immediately.

It was only when he was almost at the door of the butler's pantry that it occurred to him that this errand boy stuff was a bit *infra dig* for a vice-president, and he halted. And having halted he realized that where he ought to be was back in the drawing-room, which he should never have left, trying to break down with silver-tongued eloquence his relative's sales resistance to poor old Blister. A testing task, of course, but one not, he fancied, beyond the scope of a man who had recently played on Major R. B. and Lady Emily Finch as on a couple of stringed instruments.

Reaching the drawing-room, he found that in the brief interval since his departure Bill had left, presumably with bowed head, through the

221

French windows. But, restoring the quota of lovers to its previous level, Prudence had arrived, and her aspect showed only too plainly that she had been made acquainted with the position of affairs. Her eyes were dark with pain, and she was eating buttered toast in a crushed sort of way.

Lady Hermione was still sitting behind the teapot, as rigidly erect as if some sculptor had persuaded her to pose for his Statue of an Aunt. In all the long years during which they had been associated it seemed to Freddie that he had never seen her looking so undisguisedly the Aunt, the whole Aunt, and nothing but the Aunt, and in spite of himself his heart sank a little. Even Lady Emily Finch, though her mental outlook was that of a strong-minded mule, an animal which she resembled in features as well as temperament, had been an easier prospect.

'Blister gone?' he said, and marshalled a telling phrase or two in his mind for use later.

'Gone,' said Prudence, through a bitter mouthful of buttered toast. 'Gone without a cry. Driven into the snow before I could so much as set eyes on him. Golly, if a few people around this joint had hearts, Blandings Castle would be a better, sweeter place.'

'Well spoken, young half-portion,' said Freddie approvingly. 'I thoroughly concur. What the old dosshouse needs is a splash of the milk of human kindness. Switch it on, Aunt Hermione, is my advice.'

Lady Hermione, disregarding this appeal, asked if he had seen Beach, and Freddie said no, he had not seen Beach and he would tell her why. It was because he had hoped that better counsels would prevail, and if his aunt would give him a couple of minutes of her valuable time he would like to put forward a few arguments which might induce her to look with a kindlier eye on these young lovers who were being kept asunder.

Lady Hermione, who was somewhat addicted to homely phrases, said: 'Stuff and nonsense.' Freddie, shaking his head, said that this was hardly the spirit he had hoped to see. And Prudence, who had been sighing rather heavily at intervals, brought the names of Simon Legree and Torquemada into the conversation, speculating as to why people always made such a song and dance about their brutal inhuman inhumanity when there were others (whom she was prepared to name on request) who could give them six strokes in eighteen holes and be dormy two on the seventeenth tee.

Lady Hermione said: 'That is quite enough, Prudence,' and Freddie contested this view.

'It is not enough, Aunt Hermione. Far from it. We will now go into executive session and thresh the whole thing out. What have you got against poor old Blister? That is the question I should like to begin by asking you.'

'And this,' said Lady Hermione, 'is the question I should like to begin by asking *you*. Were you a party to this abominable trick of Galahad's?'

'Eh?'

'You know perfectly well what I mean.

Bringing that young man into the house under a false name.'

'Oh, that?' said Freddie. 'Well, I'll tell you. I was not actually help to the stratagem you mention, or I would never have dropped the brick I did. But if you are asking me: 'Am I heart and soul in Blister's cause?' the answer is in the affirmative. I consider that a union between him and this young prune here would be in the best and deepest sense a bit of all right.'

'Att-a boy, Freddie,' said the prune, well pleased with this sentiment.

'Stuff and nonsense,' said Lady Hermione, with whom it had not gone over so big. 'The man looks like a gorilla.'

'Bill does not look like a gorilla!' cried Prudence.

'Yes, he does,' said Freddie, who, though partisan, was fair. 'As far as the outer crust goes, good old Blister could walk straight into any zoo, and they would lay down the red carpet for him. But the point seems to me to have little or no bearing upon the case at issue. There is nothing in the book of rules, as far as I am aware, that prevents a man looking like a gorilla and still having what it takes when it is a question of being a good husband and a loving father, if you'll excuse me mentioning it, Prue. Just peeping into Vol. Two for a moment.'

'Quite all right,' said Prudence. 'Carry on. You're doing fine.'

'Where you have made your bloomer, Aunt Hermione, is in allowing yourself to be influenced too much by appearances. You cock an eye at Blister and you say to yourself, 'Gosh! I'd hate to meet that bird down a lonely alley on a dark night,' overlooking the fact that beneath that sinister exterior there beats one of the most outsize hearts you're likely to find in a month of Sundays. It isn't faces that matter, it's honest worth, and in that department Blister is a specialist.'

'Freddie?'

'Hullo?'

'Will you be quiet!'

'No, Aunt Hermione,' said the splendid young dog biscuit vendor stoutly. 'I will not be quiet. The time has come to speak out. Blister, as I told you before, is one of the best. And I believe I mentioned that he is the owner of a pub which only needs a bit of capital to make it a gold mine.'

Lady Hermione shuddered. She was not a woman who had ever been fond of public houses.

'The fact that this young man may have a bright future as a potboy,' she said, 'does not seem to me an argument in favour of his marrying my niece. I wish to hear no more about Mr Lister.'

The wish was not fulfilled. There was a patter of feet outside the French windows, and Gally tripped in, looking well satisfied with himself. He did not know what the European record was for a two-hundred-yard dash to a pigsty, the bribing to silence of the pig man and the two-hundred-yard dash back, but he rather fancied that he had clipped a few seconds off it. It seemed to him most improbable that in such a brief period of time anything could have gone wrong with his protégé's affairs, and the first flicker of apprehension which disturbed his equanimity came when he glanced about the room and noted his absence.

'Hullo,' he said. 'Where's Landseer?'

Lady Hermione was looking like a cook about to give notice on the evening of the big dinner party.

'If you are referring to Mr Lister, your public-house friend, he has gone.'

A deep sigh escaped Prudence.

'Aunt Hermione bunged him out, Uncle Gally.'

'What!'

'She found out who he was.'

Gally stared at his sister, stunned by this evidence of what seemed to him a scarcely human penetration.

'How the dickens,' he asked, awed, 'did you do that?'

'Freddie was obliging enough to tell me.'

Gally turned to his nephew, and his monocle shot forth flame.

'You cloth-headed young imbecile!'

It was at this point that Freddie put the two questions to which allusion has been made earlier, and followed them up with the train of reasoning which has already been outlined. He spoke eloquently and well, and as his uncle also spoke eloquently and well at the same time, a certain uproar and confusion resulted. Simultaneously Prudence was adding her mite, protesting in her clear soprano voice that she intended to marry the man she loved, no matter what anybody said and no matter how often her flinty-hearted relatives might see fit to throw the poor angel out on his ear; and Lady Hermione's position became roughly that of a chairman at a stormy meeting of shareholders.

She was endeavouring to restore order by beating on the table with a teaspoon when Veronica came in through the French windows, and at the sight of her the uproar ceased. People who knew her always stopped arguing when Veronica came along, because she was sure to want them to explain what they were arguing about and, when they had explained, to ask them to start at the beginning and explain again. And when nerves are frayed that sort of thing is annoying.

Gally stopped calling Freddie names. Freddie stopped waving his hands and appealing to the other's simple sense of justice. Prudence stopped saying they would all look pretty silly when they found her drowned in the lake one morning. And Lady Hermione stopped hammering on the table with the teaspoon. It was like a lightning strike in a boiler factory.

Veronica was radiant. Not even in the photograph taken after the Pageant in Aid of Distressed Public School Men and showing her as the Spirit of the Playing Fields of Eton had she exhibited a more boneheaded loveliness. She seemed to have developed a sort of elephantiasis of the eyes and front teeth, and her cheeks glowed with the light that never was on land or sea. She was wearing on her right wrist the best bracelet which Shrewsbury could produce at a moment's notice, and there were other ornaments on her person. But she made it plain at once that her thirst for bijouterie was by no means slaked.

'Oh, Fred-dee,' she said, 'has Uncle Clarence got back yet?'

Freddie passed a careworn hand over his brow. He had had the sense of being just about to triumph in the argument which her arrival had brought to a close, and this interruption irked him.

'Eh? Yes, the guv'nor is on the premises. You'll find him in the pigsty, I imagine.'

'Did he bring your present?'

'Oh, the present? The gift? Yes, I have it here. Here you are, with oomps and good wishes.'

'Oh, thank you, Fred-dee,' said Veronica, and withdrew into a corner to inspect it.

As a rule, as has been said, people stopped arguing when this girl came in, and they had done so now. But so gripping were the various subjects on the agenda paper that it was only a moment before the discussion broke out again. At first it was conducted in whispers, but gradually these gathered strength, until presently the boiler factory was in full swing once more.

Gally said that while he had always held a low opinion of his nephew's mentality and would never have cared to risk important money on him in an intelligence contest against a child of three with water on the brain, this latest manifestation of his ingrowing imbecility had come as a profound and painful shock, seeming, as it did, to extend the bounds of possibility. Years ago, he recalled, when shown the infant Frederick in his cradle, he had been seized by a strong conviction that the sensible thing for his parents to have done would have been to write off their losses and drown him in a bucket, and to this view he still adhered. Much misery might thus have been averted.

Freddie said that it began to look to him as if there were no such thing as justice in this world. If ever a fellow had been allowed to wander into a snare through lack of inter-office communication, that fellow was himself. Why had he not been told? Why had he not been put abreast? A simple memo would have done the trick, and no memo had been forthcoming. If the verdict of posterity was not that the whole thing was the fault of his uncle and that he himself was blameless and innocent, he would be surprised and astonished — in fact, amazed and stunned.

Prudence said that the idea of drowning herself in the lake was beginning to grow on her. It had floated into her mind just now as a rather attractive daydream, and the more she examined the project, the better it looked. She would prefer, of course, life as Mrs William Lister, but if that avenue were to be closed and poor darling Bill thrown out on the back of his neck every time he tried to get a couple of words with her, she could not see that there was anything bizarre about wanting to drown herself in the lake. It seemed to her the obvious policy to pursue. She went on to draw rather an interesting picture of

229

Lord Emsworth diving in one morning for his before-breakfast swim and bumping his head against her swollen corpse. She said it would make him think a bit, and no doubt she was right.

Lady Hermione said nothing, but continued to bang the table with the teaspoon.

What results this spoon work might eventually have produced, one cannot say. No doubt ere long the rhythmic thrumming would have influenced the tone of the discussion and done something to restore the decencies of debate. But before it had had time to make its presence felt there cut into the confused welter of competing voices a sudden observation from Veronica.

'EEEEEEEEEEE!!!' said Veronica.

The chronicler has already had occasion to show this girl saying 'EEEEEEEEEEE!!!' and it will not have been forgotten how instantaneously arresting was the effect of the word on her lips. Whatever you were doing when you heard it, your tendency was to drop it and listen.

It was so now. Gally, who had been comparing Freddie to his disadvantage with a half-witted whelk-seller whom he had met at Hurst Park the year Sandringham won the Jubilee Cup, stopped in mid-sentence. Freddie, who by way of giving some idea of what he meant by co-operation, had started to describe the filing system in vogue at the offices of Donaldson's Inc., broke off with a gasp. Prudence, who, still toying with the idea of suicide by drowning, had just remembered the notable precedent of Ophelia and was asking what Ophelia had got that she hadn't got, gave a startled jump and was silent. Lady Hermione dropped her teaspoon.

They all turned and gazed in the speaker's direction, and Freddie uttered a piercing cry.

Veronica, looking like a lovely young mother at the cot side of her newborn child, was holding aloft a superb and expensive diamond necklace.

'Oh, Fred-dee!' she said.

II

The cry which Freddie had uttered had proceeded straight from a strong man's heart. It was, as has been stated, piercing, and it had every reason to be so.

It is always exasperating for a son who has given his father the clearest possible instructions as to how to proceed in a certain matter to find that the latter has gone and got them muddled up after all, and once again, as had happened during the recent unpleasantness with his Uncle Galahad, Freddie found himself chafing at the apparent impossibility of ever obtaining co-operation in the country of his birth. He sighed for the happier conditions prevailing in the United States of northern America, where you got it at every turn.

But what had seared his soul so agonizingly when he beheld the necklace in Veronica's hands was the thought of the delay which must now inevitably ensue before it could be shipped off to Aggie. As he had explained to Prudence in their conversation in Grosvenor Square, Aggie needed the thing in a hurry. She had said so in her first wire and repeated the statement in her second, third, and fourth wires; and as the days went by and it failed to reach her, an unmistakably peevish note had crept into her communications. Niagara Threepwood (*née* Donaldson) was the sweetest of women, and there was no argument about her being the light of her husband's life and the moon of his delight, but she had inherited from her father the slightly impatient temper which led the latter at conferences to hammer on the table and shout: 'Come on, come on now!'

Thinking of the fifth wire, which might now be expected at any moment, Freddie found himself shuddering in anticipation. Going by the form book, it should be a pipterino. Even the fourth had been good, fruity stuff.

'Hell's bells!' he cried, deeply moved.

The reactions of the rest of the company to the spectacle of the glittering bauble, though differing from his in their nature, were almost equally pronounced. Gally said: 'Good Lord!' Prudence, forgetting Ophelia for the moment, said: 'Golly!' Lady Hermione said: 'Veronica! Where *did* you get that lovely necklace?'

Veronica was cooing like a dove in springtime.

'It's Freddie's present,' she explained. 'Oh, Fred-dee! How sur-*sweet* of you! I never dreamed that you meant to give me anything like this.'

It always pains a chivalrous man to be compelled to dash the cup of joy from the lips of

Beauty. The resemblance of his cousin to a young mother crooning over her new-born child had not escaped Freddie, and he was aware that what he had to say would cause chagrin and disappointment. But he did not hesitate. On these occasions the surgeon's knife is best.

'I didn't,' he said crisply. 'Not by a ruddy jugful. What you draw is a pendant.'

'A pendant?'

'A pendant,' said Freddie, who wished to leave no loophole for misunderstanding. 'It will be delivered shortly. Accept it with best wishes from the undersigned.'

Veronica's eyes widened. She seemed perplexed.

'But I'd much rather have this than a pendant. Really I would.'

'I dare say,' said Freddie, regretful but firm. 'So would most people. But that necklace happens to belong to Aggie. The story is a long and complicated one, and throws a blinding light on the guv'nor's extraordinary mentality. Boiling it down, I asked him to have the necklace mailed to Aggie in Paris and to bring back the pendant for you, and he went and got the wires crossed, though having assured me in set terms that he thoroughly understood and that there was no possibility of a hitch in the routine. I may say — and this is official — it's the last time I ever get the guv'nor to do anything for me. I believe if you sent him out to buy apples, he'd come back with an elephant.'

Lady Hermione made a noise like the hissing of fat in a saucepan.

'Isn't that Clarence!' she said, and her brother Galahad agreed that that was Clarence.

'Really,' said Lady Hermione, 'I often think he ought to be certified.'

Freddie nodded. Filial respect had prevented him putting the thought into speech, but it had crossed his mind. There were undoubtedly moments when one felt that the guv'nor's true environment was a padded cell at Colney Hatch.

'Such a disappointment for you, darling,' said Lady Hermione.

'Too bad,' said Gally.

'Tough luck, Vee,' said Prudence.

'Deepest symp,' said Freddie. 'One knows how you feel. Must be agony.'

It was only slowly that anything ever penetrated to Veronica's consciousness, and for some moments she had been standing bewildered, unable to grasp the trend of affairs. But this wave of commiseration seemed to accelerate her thought processes.

'Do you mean,' she said, beginning to understand, 'that I'm not to keep this necklace?'

Freddie replied that that was it in a nutshell.

'Can't I wear it at the County Ball?'

The question caused Lady Hermione to brighten. It seemed to her that the cup of joy need not be dashed completely from her child's lips after all. She might not be in a position to drain it to the bottom, but the arrangement she had suggested would enable her at least to take a sip or two.

'Why, of course,' she said. 'That would be lovely, darling.'

'Splendid idea,' agreed Gally. 'Compromise satisfactory to all parties. Wear it at the County Ball, and then turn it in and Freddie can ship it off.'

'You'll look wonderful in it, Vee,' said Prudence. 'I shan't be there to see you, because I shall have drowned myself in the lake, but I know you'll look marvellous.'

Once more Freddie was reluctantly compelled to apply the surgeon's knife.

'Imposs, I fear,' he said, with a manly pity that became him well. 'I'm sorry, Vee, old girl, but that idea's out too. The jamboree to which you allude does not take place for another fortnight, and Aggie wants the thing at once. She has already wired four times for it, and I am expecting telegram number five to-morrow or the day after. And I don't mind telling you that it promises to be hot stuff. At the thought of what she would say if I kept her waiting another fortnight the imagination boggles.'

The Hon. Galahad snorted sharply. Himself a bachelor, he was unable to understand and sympathize with what seemed to him a nephew's contemptible pusillanimity. There is often this unbridgable gulf between the outlook of single and married men.

'Are you afraid of your wife?' he demanded. 'Are you man or mouse? She can't eat you.'

'She'd have a jolly good try,' said Freddie. 'What you don't appear to realize is that Aggie is the daughter of an American millionaire, and if you'd ever met an American millionaire — '

'I've met dozens.'

'Then you ought to know that they bring their daughters up to expect a certain docility in the male. Aggie got the idea into her nut at about the age of six that her word was law and never lost it, and it was always understood that there was a sort of gentleman's agreement that the bird who married her would roll over and jump through hoops on demand. There are few, if any, sweeter girls on earth than good old Aggie, but if you ask me: 'Is she a bit on the imperious side from time to time?' I answer frankly that you have rung the bell and are entitled to the cigar or coco-nut. I love her with a devotion which defies human speech, but if you were to place before me the alternatives of disregarding her lightest behest and walking up to a traffic cop and socking him on the maxillary bone, you would find me choosing the cop every time. And it's no good calling me a bally young serf,' said Freddie, addressing the Hon. Galahad, who had done so. 'That's the posish, and I like it. I fully understood what I was letting myself in for when the registrar was doing his stuff.'

There was a silence. It was broken by Veronica making a suggestion.

'You could tell Aggie you had lent the necklace to me.'

'I could,' agreed Freddie, 'and I would if I wanted hell's foundations to quiver and something like the San Francisco earthquake to break loose. You all seem to have overlooked another important point, which, though delicate, I can touch on as we're all members of the family here. Some silly ass went and told Aggie that Vee and I were once engaged, and ever since she has viewed Vee with concern. She suspects her every move.'

'Ridiculous!' said Lady Hermione. 'A mere boy-and-girl affair.'

'Blew over years ago,' said Gally.

'I dare say,' said Freddie. 'But to listen to Aggie, when the topic crops up, you'd think it had happened yesterday. So I'm jolly well not going to lend you that necklace, Vee, and I will now ask you — regretfully, and fully appreciating your natural disappointment and all that sort of thing — to look slippy and hand it over.'

'Oh, Fred-dee!'

'I'm sorry, but there you are. That's life.'

Veronica's hand stole out. There was a quiver on her lovely lips and moisture in her beautiful eyes, but her hand holding the necklace stole out. When a man trained in eloquence in the testing school of Donaldson's Inc. of Long Island City employs that eloquence at its full voltage, it is enough to make any girl's hand steal out.

'Thanks,' said Freddie.

He had spoken too soon. It was as if some sudden vision of the County Ball had come to Veronica Wedge, with herself in the foreground feeling practically naked without those shining diamonds about her neck. Her lips ceased to quiver and set in a firm and determined line. The moisture left her eyes, to be replaced by a fanatic gleam of defiance. She drew back her hand.

'No,' she said.

'Eh?' said Freddie weakly.

237

A strange bonelessness had come upon him. The situation was one which he had not anticipated, and he was asking himself how he was going to cope with it. The man of sentiment cannot leap at girls and choke necklaces out of them.

'No,' repeated Veronica. 'You gave me this as a birthday present and I'm going to keep it.'

'Keep it? You don't mean absolutely freeze on to it permanently?'

'Yes, I do.'

'But it's Aggie's!'

'She can buy another.'

This happy solution restored Lady Hermione's composure completely.

'Of course she can. How sensible of you, darling. I'm surprised you didn't think of that, Freddie.'

'Sounds to me an admirable way out,' agreed Gally. 'You can always get round these difficulties if you use your head.'

Freddie's was now reeling as it had not reeled since those bygone nights with Tipton Plimsoll in his pre-Jimpson Murgatroyd period, but he endeavoured to make these people see the light of reason. It amazed him that nobody seemed to realize the spot he was in.

'But don't you understand? Didn't you grasp what I was saying just now? Aggie will go up in the air like a rocket when she hears I've given Vee — Vee of all people! — her necklace. She'll divorce me.'

'Nonsense.'

'She will, I tell you. American wives are like

that. Let the slightest thing ruffle their equanimity, and *bingo*! Ask Tippy. His mother divorced his guv'nor because he got her to the station at ten-seven to catch a train that had started at seven-ten.'

The Hon. Galahad's eye lit up.

'That reminds me of a rather amusing story — '

But the story of which he had been reminded was not to be told on this occasion — though, knowing Gally, one cannot believe that it was lost to the world for ever. A sharp cough from his sister drew his attention to the fact that Tipton Plimsoll was entering the room.

III

Tipton was unmistakably effervescent, his manner and appearance alike completely exploding his hostess's theory that he must be exhausted after his long drive. His spectacles were gleaming, and he seemed to float on air.

There is a widely advertised patent medicine which promises to its purchasers a wonderful sense of peace, poise, neural solidity and organic integrity, and guarantees to free them from all nervous irritability, finger-drumming, teeth-grinding, and foot-tapping. This specific Tipton Plimsoll might have been taking for weeks, and the poet Coleridge, had he been present, would have jerked a thumb at him with a low-voiced: 'Don't look now, but that fellow over there will give you some idea of what I had in mind when

I wrote about the man who on honeydew had fed and drunk the milk of Paradise.'

'Hi, ya!' he cried, the first time he had used the expression in Blandings Castle.

But it has been well said that it is precisely these moments when we are feeling that ours is the world and everything that's in it that Fate selects for sneaking up on us with the rock in the stocking. Scarcely had Tipton floated half a dozen feet when he was brought up short by the sight of Veronica dandling the necklace, and it was as if a blunt instrument had descended on the base of his skull.

'What's that?' he cried, tottering. He did not actually clutch his brow, but anyone could have seen that it was a very near thing. 'Who gave you that?' he demanded tensely.

Lady Hermione awoke to a sudden sense of peril. She had not forgotten the night of her wealthy future son-in-law's arrival at the castle and his strongly-marked reaction to the spectacle of Veronica slapping Freddie on the wrist and telling him not to be so silly, and the look of quick suspicion which he had just cast at the last named told her that he still feared his fatal fascination. Let him learn that this ornate piece of jewellery was a gift from Freddie and who knew what horrors might not ensue? A vision of the owner of the controlling interest in Tipton's Stores stalking out, leaving a broken engagement behind him, made her feel for a moment quite faint.

She was wondering how, without actually drawing her into a corner and slowly and carefully explaining to her for about forty minutes, She could impress upon her child the absolutely vital necessity for secrecy and evasion, when Veronica spoke.

'Freddie gave it me for my birthday,' she said.

From Tipton's lips, starting from the lower reaches of his soul, there came a low, soft, hollow, grunting sound. Lord Emsworth, had he been there to hear, would have recognized it as familiar. It closely resembled the noise which sometimes proceeded from the Empress when she was trying to get a potato which had rolled beyond her reach. He tottered again, more noticeably than the first time.

'Yes, Tip-pee.'

When we last saw Tipton Plimsoll, he was, it will be remembered, all straightened out on the snake question. The frank delight with which Freddie had received the news of his engagement and the hearty manner in which he had shaken his hand had finally dispelled the uneasy suspicions which had been oppressing him for so long. We faded out, it will be recalled, on a medium shot of him erasing the young dog biscuiteer's name from his list of snakes and according to him the honourable status of an innocent cousin.

Now, his heart sinking till it seemed to be all mixed up with his socks, he saw that the slitherer, when exhibiting joy at the news of his engagement, had been but acting a part. The handshake which he had mistaken for that of a pal had been the handshake of a serpent, and of a serpent who had, the moment his back was turned, intended to go on playing the old army game with the girl he loved. No wonder Tipton tottered. Anyone would have tottered.

It was the licentious lavishness of the gift that made the whole ghastly set-up so hideously plain. If Freddie had presented Veronica with a modest wrist watch or a simple pendant, he would have had no criticism to make. Quite in order, he would have said, as from cousin to cousin. But a necklace that must have cost a packet was a very different matter. Cousins do not blow their substance on expensive diamond necklaces and give them to girls on their birthdays. Snakes, in sharp contradistinction, do.

'Cheese!' he muttered, using this expression, too, for the first time on these refined premises.

Freddie, meanwhile, had paled beneath his tan. He could read what was passing in Tipton's mind as clearly as if it had been the top line on an oculist's chart, and the thought that unless prompt steps were taken through the proper channels the exclusive concession which the other, speaking for Tipton's Stores, had granted to Donaldson's Dog-Joy might go west chilled him to the marrow.

'It's my wife's!' he cried.

He would have done better to remain silent. The cynical confession set the seal on Tipton's horror and disgust. For while we may pardon, if only with difficulty, the snake which seeks to undermine a young girl's principles at its own expense, at the snake which swipes its wife's jewellery as a means to this end we look askance, and rightly.

'What I mean — '

A smooth voice cut in on Freddie's broken stammer. It was the voice of one whose suave diplomacy had a hundred times reconciled brawling race-course touts and acted like oil upon troubled waters when feelings ran high between jellied-eel sellers.

'Just a moment, Freddie.'

The Hon. Galahad's was essentially a kindly soul. He was a man who liked to see everybody happy and comfortable. It had not escaped his notice that his sister Hermione was looking like an interested bystander waiting for a time bomb to explode, and it seemed to him that the moment had arrived for a polished man of the world to take the situation in hand.

'What Freddie is trying to say, my dear fellow, is that the thing originally belonged to his wife. Having no more use for it, she handed it over to him to do what he liked with. Why should there be anything to cause remark in the fact that he gave the little trinket to Veronica?'

Tipton stared.

'You call that a little trinket? It must have cost ten thousand smackers.'

'Ten thousand smackers?' There was genuine amusement in the Hon. Galahad's jolly laugh. 'My dear chap! Don't tell me you've got the idea into your mind that it's real? As if any man with Freddie's scrupulous sense of the fitness of things would go giving a ten-thousand-dollar necklace to a girl who has just become engaged to his friend. There are some things that are not done. Mrs Freddie bought that necklace at the five-and-ten-cent store. Or did I misunderstand you when you told me that, Freddie?'

'Perfectly correct, Uncle Gally.'

Tipton's brow became wrinkled.

'She bought it at the five-and-ten-cent store?'

'That's right.'

'Just for a gag, you mean?'

'Exactly. A woman's whim. I wonder if you have ever heard the one about the man whose wife had a whim of iron? He was going down the street one day — '

Tipton was not interested in men with iron-whimmed wives. He was pondering on this new angle and finding the explanation plausible. He had known wealthy female compatriots of his to buy some odd things. Doris Jimpson had once bought twelve coloured balloons, and they had popped them with their cigarettes on the way home in the car. His sombre face began to clear, and one noted a relaxation in the tenseness of his bearing.

It was unfortunate, therefore, that Veronica should have chosen this moment to give tongue. You could generally rely on Veronica to say the wrong thing, and she did so now.

'I'm going to wear it at the County Ball, Tip-pee.'

An instant before, it had seemed as though Tipton Plimsoll were about to become again the carefree soul who had entered the room with a merry 'Hi, ya!' His eye, resting on Freddie, had not had actual brotherly love in it, but it had been reasonably free from horrified suspicion and loathing disgust and seemed likely to

244

become freer. The caveman in Tipton Plimsoll, you would have said, was preparing to put up the shutters and close down.

But at these words his brow darkened once more and a haughty gleam shot from his horn-rimmed spectacles. Veronica had touched his pride.

'Is that so?' he said formidably. 'Wear it at the County Ball, huh? You think I'm going to have my future wife wearing fake five-and-ten-cent store jewellery at any by golly County Ball? I'll say I'm not. I'm the fellow who'll buy you all the stuff you need for the County Ball. Me!' said Tipton, pointing with his left hand at his torso and with his right jerking the necklace from her grasp.

'Hey!' he said.

His eye, sweeping the room, had fallen on Prudence. Wearying of a discussion whose din and uproar were preventing her thinking of lakes, she had begun to move towards the door.

'You off?'

'I am going to my room,' said Prudence.

Tipton stopped her with an imperious gesture.

'Juss-a-moment. You were saying yesterday you needed something for that jumble sale of yours. Take this,' said Tipton.

'Right ho,' said Prudence listlessly. 'Thanks.'

She passed through the door, leaving a throbbing silence behind her.

IV

Prudence's room was at the back of the castle, next door to Tipton Plimsoll's. Its balcony

245

looked down on meadows and trees, and so a few minutes later did Prudence. For on leaving the drawing-room she had gone to lean on the rail, her sad eyes roaming over the spreading woodland, her bruised spirit seeking to obtain some solace from the contemplation of the peaceful scene. She eyed the copses and spinneys from much the same general motives as had led Tipton on a memorable occasion to go and look at the ducks on the Serpentine.

But when a spirit is as bruised as hers, there is not much percentage in gazing at scenery. Presently she went back into the room with a weary sigh, which changed abruptly to a startled squeak. She had seen a human form sitting in the armchair, and it had made her jump.

'Hullo, my dear,' said her Uncle Galahad genially. 'I saw you out there but didn't like to disturb you. Your air was that of a girl deep in meditation. Did you think I was a burglar?'

'I thought you were Freddie.'

'Do I look like Freddie?' said Gally, wounded.

'I thought it was Freddie come for the necklace.'

There was a grave expression on Gally's face as he adjusted his monocle and focused it upon her.

'It is extremely fortunate that it wasn't, considering that you had left the thing lying right out in the open on your dressing-table. You might have ruined everything. Oh, it's all right now. I've got it in my pocket. Don't you realize, my dear child, what the possession of this necklace means to you?'

Prudence made a tired gesture, like a Christian martyr who has got a bit fed up with lions.

'It doesn't mean anything to me. Nothing means anything to me if I can't have Bill.'

Gally rose and patted her on the head. It meant leaving the armchair, which was a very comfortable one, but he did it. A man with a big heart is always ready to put up with discomfort when it is a case of consoling a favourite niece. At the same time he regarded her with frank astonishment. He had supposed her mind to be nimbler than this.

'You're going to have Bill,' he said. 'I fully expect to be dancing at your wedding at an early date. Haven't you grasped the position of affairs yet? Why, you might be Veronica.'

'What do you mean?'

'This necklace is the talisman which is going to unlock the gates of happiness for you. Freeze on to it like flypaper and refuse to give it up no matter what threats and cajoleries may be employed, and all you will have to worry about is where to spend the honeymoon. Can't you understand that you have been handed the whole situation on a plate? What's going to happen when you refuse to part with this necklace? The opposition will have to come to terms, and we shall dictate those terms.'

The Hon. Galahad removed his monocle, breathed on it, polished it with his handkerchief, and put it back.

'Let me tell you,' he said, 'what happened after you left the drawing-room. Plimsoll took

Veronica off for a stroll, leaving the rest of us to our general meeting. Freddie was the first to take the floor. He told us rather eloquently what Aggie was going to do to him if she didn't get her necklace. His speech was accorded only a rather tepid reception. Your Aunt Hermione seemed to think that the disaster to which he alluded was exclusively Freddie's headache. My ready wit had saved the situation, leaving Plimsoll soothed and happy, and that was all she cared about. As far as she was concerned, the incident was closed.'

'Well, wasn't it?'

'It might have been, if Freddie had not ripped it wide open again. America's done something to that boy. It's made him think on his feet and get constructive ideas. This time he held his audience spellbound.'

'What did he say?'

'I'll tell you. He threatened, unless the necklace was in his hands by nightfall, to blow the gaff. He said he would tell Plimsoll what it was really worth and add that he had given it to Veronica as a birthday present and leave the rest to him. He said that this would probably mean the loss of some concession or other which Plimsoll had promised him, but that if he was going to have a headache he intended others to share it with him. His remarks caused a sensation. I don't think I have ever seen Hermione so purple. She is convinced that if Plimsoll ever finds out that necklace is genuine he will break off the engagement and stalk out of Veronica's life. It appears that he is madly jealous of Freddie.'

Prudence gave an awed gasp.

'Golly!' she said. 'I see what you mean.'

'I thought you would. Hermione's anguish was painful to witness, and Clarence, who dropped in with your Uncle Egbert just in time to join the conference at this point, put the lid on it by revealing that he had told young Plimsoll that Freddie and Veronica were once engaged. He said Egbert had told him to. Egbert says he told him *not* to. I left them arguing the point.'

Prudence's eyes had rolled to the ceiling. She seemed to be offering silent thanks to Heaven for a notable display of benevolence to a damsel in distress.

'But, Uncle Gally, this is marvellous!'

'Solves everything.'

'They'll have to let me marry Bill.'

'Exactly. That is our price. We stick to it.'

'We won't weaken.'

'Not an iota. If they come bothering you, refer them to your agent. Tell them I've got the thing.'

'But then they'll bother you.'

'My dear child, mine has been a long life, in the course of which I have frequently been bothered by experts. And always without effect. Bothering passes me by as the idle wind, which I respect not.'

'That's Shakespeare, isn't it?'

'I shouldn't wonder. Most of the good gags are.'

Prudence drew a deep breath.

'You're a great man to have on one's side, Uncle Gally.'

'I like to stick up for my pals.'

'What a bit of luck Bill getting you for a godfather.'

'So I said at the time. There was a school of thought which held otherwise. Well, I'm going to my room to hide the swag.'

'Hide it carefully.'

'I'll put it in a place where no one would dream of looking. After that I thought of going for a saunter in the cool of the evening. Care to join me?'

'I'd love to, but I've got to write to Bill. I say, Uncle Gally,' said Prudence, struck with a sudden thought. 'All this is a bit tough on Freddie, isn't it?'

The same thing had occurred to the Hon. Galahad. 'A little, I suppose. Possibly just a trifle. But you can't make an omelette without breaking eggs. Not Shakespeare,' said the Hon. Galahad. 'One of my own. Unless I heard it somewhere. Besides, Freddie's agony will be only temporary. Hermione will have to throw in the towel. No alternative. I told her so in set terms, and left her to think it over.'

10

I

If Prudence had had keener ears — or, rather, if her hearing had not at the moment been dulled by grief- she might have heard, while leaning on the rail of her balcony, a sound from below which would have registered itself on her consciousness as a gasping cry. And if she had been looking more narrowly at the meadows and spinneys — if, that is to say, her eyes had not been blurred with unshed tears — she would have noticed that it proceeded from Bill Lister, who was sitting on a tree stump outside the second spinney to the right.

But being preoccupied she missed him, and Bill, who had sprung to his feet and was about to start waving his arms like a semaphore in the hope of attracting her attention, had the chagrin of seeing her vanish like some goddess in a dream. The best he was able to do was to take careful note of the spot at which she had made her brief appearance and go off to see if he could find a ladder.

In supposing that Bill had left the drawing-room with bowed head during his absence, Freddie had been quite correct. After a rather one-sided exchange of remarks with Lady Hermione he had seen that there was nothing to keep him, and pausing only to knock over a chair and upset the cake table again he had tottered forth into the sunshine. Any anxiety he might have felt about the disposition of his luggage was dispelled by his hostess's assurance that it would be thrown out after him and would in due course find its way to the Emsworth Arms.

The emotions of a man who, arriving at a country house for a long visit, finds himself kicked out at the end of the first twenty minutes are necessarily chaotic, but on one point Bill was pretty clear — that he had plenty of time on his hands. It was not yet six o'clock, and the day seemed to stretch before him endlessly. By way of getting through it somehow he started on a desultory tour of the grounds, and instinctively avoiding those in the front of the house, where the danger of running into Lady Hermione again would be more acute, he had come at length to the second spinney on the right of Prudence's balcony. There he had sat down to review his position and to endeavour to assess his chances of ever seeing again the girl he loved.

And such is the whimsicality of Fortune that he had seen her again within the first couple of minutes. True, she had come and gone like something out of a cuckoo clock, but he had seen her. And, as we say, he had marked the spot carefully and gone off to find a ladder.

That his mind should have turned so immediately in the direction of ladders is not really surprising. Romeo's would have done the same, and so, if the Hon. Galahad's diagnosis of his temperament had been a correct one, would that of Tipton Plimsoll's Uncle Chet. Uncle

Chet, like Romeo, had been a man who thought on his feet and did it now when there were girls around, and Bill was as full of ardour and impetuosity as either of them. The primary impulse of every lover, on seeing the adored object on a balcony, is to shin up and join her.

One of the things which may be placed to the credit side of the English country house is that if you want a ladder when you are in its grounds, you can generally find one. It may take time, as it did on this occasion, but the search is seldom fruitless. Bill eventually found his propped up against a tree, where somebody seemed to have been doing a bit of pruning, and it was here that his powerful physique, which had been of such negligible value to him in the interior of Barribault's Hotel and, for the matter of that, in the Blandings Castle drawing-room, began to show returns. A ladder, even the medium-sized one which he had found, is not a light burden, but he made nothing of it. He carried it like a clouded cane. There were moments when he came near to flicking it.

He placed it against the wall, steadied it, and began to climb. Love lent him wings. Massive though he was, he skimmed up the rungs like a featherweight. He reached the balcony. He hurried into the room. And down below Colonel Egbert Wedge, who at the conclusion of the general meeting had decided that only a brisk walk could restore a mental poise rudely shaken by his exchanges with Lord Emsworth, rounded the corner of the house and stood staring.

The impression left on Colonel Wedge's mind

by the general meeting, and particularly by his brother-in-law's share in it, had been that he had already undergone the maximum which a retired colonel of a cavalry unit could reasonably be expected to endure. If you had buttonholed him as he stalked out of the drawing-room and said to him: 'Tell me, Colonel Wedge, have you drained the bitter cup?' he would have replied: 'Yes, dash it, certainly. To the dregs.' And now, on top of all that, here was a beastly bounder of a burglar having the cool effrontery to break into the house in broad daylight.

It was this that was causing his blood pressure to rise in a manner which would have made E. Jimpson Murgatroyd shake his head. At night, yes. He could have understood that. If this had happened in the small hours or even round about the time of the final whisky and soda, he might not actually have approved of the blasted fellow's activities, but he could have put himself to a certain extent in his place. But at a moment when the household had not yet digested its five-o'clock tea and buttered toast . . .

'Tchsh!' said Colonel Wedge, revolted, and gave the ladder a petulant jerk.

It measured its length on the turf, and he hurried off to G.H.Q. to put in his report and make arrangements for reinforcements.

II

After the departure of her Uncle Galahad, Prudence had not lingered long in her room. A girl in love, remorseful for having wounded the man of her choice and pouring out her heart to him with a fountain pen, writes nearly as quickly as Lord Emsworth sending off telegrams at Paddington Station with his train puffing in the background. She had finished the letter and addressed it to W. Lister, Esq., at the Emsworth Arms and licked the gum and fastened it up long before Bill had come anywhere near his ladder.

It was her intention to get in touch with one of the under housemaids with whom she had struck up an acquaintance, warm enough perhaps to be called a friendship, and to fee her to take it down by hand after dinner; and she set out now to find her.

And so it came about that Bill, entering the room with beating heart, found it empty and was for an instant downcast.

But a moment later he had perceived that though he had missed Prudence, he had found the next best thing. The letter was lying on the dressing-table, where its author had thought it wisest to leave it while she conducted her negotiations with the under housemaid. In the present unsettled conditions at Blandings Castle, to have taken it with her would have been too much like carrying despatches through the enemy's lines in war-time.

It was with trembling fingers that Bill opened the envelope. In the course of their romantic love affair he had received in all forty-seven letters from this girl, but while the sight of her handwriting had always affected him powerfully, it had never affected him so powerfully as now.

So much hung on this communication. The other forty-six had been mere variations on the theme 'I love you,' and very pleasant reading they had made! But this one — the room swam before him as the thought shot through his soul like a red-hot skewer — might quite possibly be the bird. It was the answer to his well-expressed note pleading for a reconciliation, and who knew what scornful rebuffs it might not contain?

Through the mist which flickered before his eyes he read the words

My own precious darling beautiful Bill

and he felt as he had sometimes felt on stricken football fields when a number of large, well-fed members of the opposition team had risen from their seat on his stomach. Reason told him that a girl whose intention it was to rebuff and to administer the bird would scarcely have chosen this preamble.

'Woof!' he breathed, and with swelling heart settled down to a steady perusal.

It was a wonderful letter. Indeed, off-hand, he did not see how it could well have been improved upon. Its gist was that she loved him as of yore — in fact, even more than of yore. She made that clear in paragraph one, and clearer still in the pages which followed. She was, indeed, so complimentary about him that somebody like Lady Hermione, had she perused the eulogy, would have supposed that there was some mistake and that she must be thinking of a couple of other fellows. Even Bill, though he had read the same sort of thing forty-six times before, found a difficulty in realizing that this godlike being whose virtues provoked such enthusiasm in her was himself.

On page four the tone of the letter changed. At first a mere outpouring of worship and affection, it now became more like some crisp despatch from the Front. For it was here that the writer began to outline for his attention the saga of the necklace. And, as he read, his heart bounded within him. So clearly had she set forth the salient points that he was able to follow the scenario step by step to its triumphant conclusion without any difficulty, and he recognized that what had happened was what Freddie would have called in the best and deepest sense a bit of all right. Rout had been turned to victory.

The thought did strike him, as it had struck Prudence, that it was all perhaps a bit tough on Freddie, who seemed through no fault of his own to have become a sort of football of Fate; but it was not long before he was consoling himself with the philosophical reflection which had enabled the Hon. Galahad to bear up — viz., that the breaking of eggs is an inseparable adjunct to the making of omelettes and that in any case his old friend's agony would be only temporary. 'Hermione,' Gally had said, 'will have to throw in the towel,' and this was the bracing conclusion to which Bill, too, came. It would have been difficult at this moment for anything to have increased his happiness.

But something now happened which definitely

diminished it. From outside in the corridor there came the sudden sound of voices, and he leaped up and stood rigid, listening.

Nor was his agitation without reason. One of the voices was that of Lady Hermione Wedge, and such had been his relations with her that her lightest word was enough to make him tremble.

'Are you sure?' she was saying.

The voice which replied was strange to Bill, for he had not yet had the privilege of meeting Colonel Wedge.

'Quite sure, old girl. No possibility of error. He propped a beastly great ladder against the wall, and before my very eyes he shinned up it like a lamplighter. I can show you the ladder. Here, come and look. Down there.'

There was an interval of silence, during which the unseen speakers had apparently gone to gaze out of one of the corridor windows. Then Lady Hermione spoke.

'Most extraordinary,' she said. 'Yes, I see the ladder.'

'He climbed up to a bally balcony,' said Colonel Wedge, like some member of the Capulet family speaking of Romeo.

'And he can't have climbed down.'

'Exactly. And if he had come down the stairs, we should have met him. We arrive, then, at the irresistible conclusion that the bounder is lurking in one of these rooms, and I shall now search them one by one.'

'Oh, Egbert, no!'

'Eh? Why not? I've got my service revolver.'

'No. You might get hurt. Wait till Charles and

258

Thomas come. They ought to have been here long ago.'

'Well, all right. After all, there's no hurry. The blighter can't get away. One can proceed at one's leisure.'

In every difficult situation, when the spirit has been placed upon the rack and peril seems to threaten from every quarter, there inevitably comes soon or late to the interested party at the centre of the proceedings a conviction that things are getting too hot. Stags at bay have this feeling. So have Red Indians at the stake. It came now to Bill.

Who Charles and Thomas might be, he did not know. As a matter of fact, they were respectively the Blandings Castle first and second footmen. We saw them before, it may be remembered, toiling into the drawing-room with cream and powdered sugar. They were now restoring their tissues in the Servants' Hall and listening without enthusiasm to the details of the assignment which was being sketched out for them by Beach, the butler. The delay in their arrival was owing to the slowness with which Beach was putting across the idea which he was trying to sell them; they holding, properly enough, that it was not their place to go and overpower burglars right in the middle of their meat tea.

To Bill, as we say, their names were unfamiliar; but whoever they were, and however long they might take in reaching the front line, it seemed pretty clear to him that they might be expected eventually, and he had no desire to remain and make their acquaintance. It was not that a man of his thews and courage shrank from a turn-up with a hundred Charleses and Thomases, any more than he paled at the menace of a thousand colonels with service revolvers. What urged him to retreat was the thought of having to meet Lady Hermione again. It stimulated him to action like a cactus in the trouser seat.

Having decided to leave, his first move was to lock the door so as to ensure himself at least a respite when the big push started. This done, he hastened out on to the balcony.

It had been Colonel Wedge's view that there was no need for hurry, because the blighter could not get away, and Bill would have been the first to acknowledge that the loss of the ladder had struck a very serious blow at his line of communications. But that he was actually encircled he would have disputed. What the colonel had not allowed for was the extraordinary stimulus which the prospect of having to meet his wife gave to blighters' mental powers. The brain of a blighter faced with the imminent prospect of an encounter with a woman of the type of Lady Hermione Wedge works like lightning, and it was almost no time before Bill was telling himself that on the walls of houses there are generally water pipes down which a venturesome man may slide.

A moment later he had seen one. And as his eye, sweeping the castle wall, fell upon it, his stout heart sank. It was a matter of some dozen feet away from him.

To a performing flea, of course, a standing

broad jump of a dozen feet would have been child's play. Such a flea in Bill's place would have bowed to the audience, smiled at personal friends in the front row, dusted off its antenna and made the leap with a careless 'Allay-oop!' Bill did not even contemplate its possibility. He knew his limitations. There was once a young man on the flying trapeze who flew through the air with the greatest of ease, but he had presumably had years of training. Bill was a novice.

It was as he stood there with a silent 'What to do?' on his lips that he suddenly saw that there was still hope. Running along the wall was a narrow ledge. Furthermore, Blandings Castle having been in existence a great number of years, ivy had grown upon its surface in some profusion. And a man anxious to remove himself from a balcony here to a water pipe over there can do a great deal with the assistance of a ledge and some ivy.

What held Bill motionless for a while, wrinkling his forehead and chewing the lower lip a little, was a growing doubt as to whether he wanted to be that man. There was a pleasantly solid look about that ivy; its strands were stout and gnarled and certainly had the appearance of being strong enough to support him; but you can never be quite sure about ivy. It puts up an impressive front and then, just when it is the time for all good ivy to come to the aid of the party, it lets you down. That was the thought which was causing Bill to hesitate. Like Freddie, he yearned for co-operation, and he wanted to be quite certain that he was going to get it.

There was no question that failure on the part of that ivy to give one-hundred-per-cent service would mean a quick, sticky finish for the man who had put his trust in it. He would go straight down and not stop till he had hit the lawn, and it did not escape Bill's notice that that lawn had a hard, unyielding look. He could see himself bouncing — once, twice, possibly thrice — and then lying lifeless, like the man in 'Excelsior'.

He was still weighing the pros and cons when there cut abruptly into his meditations the sound of a woman's voice, sharpened by the excitement of the chase.

'This door is locked. He must be in here. Break down this door, Charles.'

Worse things can happen to a man than lying lifeless on lawns. Bill scrambled over the balcony rail and set his foot on the ledge.

Simultaneously, Tipton Plimsoll hurried past the group in the corridor and shot into his bedroom like a homing rabbit.

III

Tipton lowered himself into a chair with a satisfied grunt, his air that of a man glad to be at journey's end. He was breathing a little jerkily, for he had come up the stairs at a smart pace. A spectator, had one been present, would have observed that beneath his coat there was some bulky object, spoiling the set of it. It was as if he had grown a large tumour on his left side.

At about the moment when Bill, having heard all he wanted to hear on the subject of Charleses, Thomases, and service revolvers, retreated to the balcony and started looking around for water pipes, Tipton had been leaving the Hon. Galahad's suite on the ground floor in the furtive manner of a stag which, while not yet actually at bay, is conscious of a certain embarrassment and a desire to avoid attention. He had been to fetch the flask which he had been mad enough to allow out of his possession, foolishly overlooking the fact that the time was bound to come when he would need it, and need it sorely.

It was the presence of this flask on his person which had caused him to whizz so nimbly past the group in the corridor. He had seen that the gathering consisted of Colonel Wedge, Lady Hermione Wedge, Beach, the butler, and a brace of footmen, and at any other time — for the affair undoubtedly presented certain features of interest — he would have paused to ask questions. But with that bulge under his coat he shrank from establishing communication with his fellows, who might ask questions in their turn. The fact that this assorted mob was gathered about the door next to his own and seemed to be gazing at it with great intentness filled him not with curiosity but with thankfulness. It meant that their backs were turned, thus enabling him to pass by unseen.

Safe in his refuge, he now produced the flask, looking at it with affection and an anticipatory gleam in his eye. His manner had ceased to betray anxiety and embarrassment. If he still resembled a stag, it was a stag at eve, about to drink its fill. His tongue stole out and passed lightly over his lips.

In the period which had passed since he last appeared on the Blandings scene a complete change had taken place in Tipton Plimsoll's mood. He had quite got over that momentary spasm of bad temper which had led him to snatch the necklace from Veronica's grasp and fling it scornfully to Prudence as a contribution towards the vicar's jumble sale. Five minutes in the rose garden with the girl he loved had made another man of him.

He was now filled to the brim with a benevolence so wide in its scope that it even embraced Freddie. He had got back to his old idea of Freddie as a man and a brother, and was glad he had given him that concession for his blasted dog biscuits. He saw that he had wronged Freddie. After all, it is surely straining a regard for the proprieties absurdly to object to a male cousin giving a female cousin a trifle of five-and-ten-cent store jewellery on her birthday.

But there were other and weightier reasons for his desire to celebrate than a mere conviction of the blamelessness of one whom he had once been reluctantly compelled to class among the rattlesnakes and black mambas. Apart from the intoxicating feeling of being betrothed to the only girl in the world, there was the realization that he had passed through the valley of the shadow and come up smiling on the other side. Even E. Jimpson Murgatroyd would now be compelled in common honesty to give him a clean bill of health.

For mark what had happened. In order to brace himself up to tell his love he had taken a snifter. And what had ensued? He had seen a pig in a bedroom. Yes, but a real pig, a genuine pig, a pig that was equally visible to such unbiased eyes as those of Veronica and her mother. E. Jimpson Murgatroyd himself in his place would have seen precisely what he had seen. No amount of quibbling on his part could get around that.

And another thing which must have impressed E. J. Murgatroyd very deeply, had he been apprised of it, was that from start to finish there had not been a sign of the face. For the first time in his association with it, it had been subjected to the test and had failed to deliver.

To what conclusion, then, was one forced? One was forced to the conclusion that he had turned the corner. The pure air of Shropshire had done its work, and he was now cured and in a position to go ahead and drink to his happiness as it should be drunk to.

And he was proceeding to do so when he saw something out of the corner of his eye and, turning, realized that he had underestimated the face's tenacity and will to win. What had kept it away earlier this afternoon he could not say — some appointment elsewhere, perhaps; but in light-heartedly assuming that it had retired from business he had been sadly mistaken.

There it was, pressed against the windowpane, that same fixed, intent expression in its eyes. It seemed to be trying to say something to him.

IV

The reason Bill's eyes were fixed and intent was that the sight of Tipton through the window had come to him like that of a sail on the horizon to a shipwrecked mariner. And what he was trying to say to him was that he would be glad if Tipton would at his earliest convenience open the window and let him in.

There is this about climbing along ledges towards water pipes, that by the time you have reached your water pipe and have come to the point where you are going to slide down it the whole idea of sliding down water pipes is apt to have lost any charm which it may have possessed at the outset of your journey. Bill, facing the last leg of his trip, was feeling the same lack of faith in the trustworthiness of the water pipe as he had formerly felt in that of the ivy.

Arriving at the window, therefore, and seeing Tipton, he decided abruptly to alter his whole scheme of campaign. He had recognized the other immediately as the tall, thin chap who had showed himself so aloof on the occasion of their encounter in the rhododendrons, but he was hoping that in the special circumstances he might be induced to unbend a bit. In Tipton he saw one of those men who dislike talking to strangers and raise their eyebrows and pass on if accosted by them; but, after all, when it is a question of saving a human life, the aloofest of tall, thin chaps may reasonably be expected to stretch a point.

What he wanted Tipton to do was to let him in

and allow him to remain in modest seclusion under the bed or somewhere until the fever of the chase had spent itself in the bosoms of Charles, whoever he was, of Thomas, whoever *he* was, of the unidentified person with the service revolver, and of Lady Hermione. He did not want to talk to Tipton or bore him in any way, and he was prepared to give him a guarantee that he would not dream of presuming on this enforced acquaintance. He was perfectly willing that Tipton, if he desired to do so, should cut him next time they met, provided that he would extend the hand of assistance now.

It was a difficult idea to put through a closed window, but by way of starting the negotiations he placed his lips to the pane and said:

'Hi!'

He could have made no more unfortunate move. Recalling as it did so strongly to Tipton the circumstances of their last meeting, the monosyllable set the seal on the latter's gloom and depression. Bill did not, of course, know it, but it was that 'Hi!' of his at their previous encounter which had affected the man behind the flask even more powerfully than the mere sight of his face. Broadly, what Tipton felt about phantom faces was that a man capable of taking the rough with the smooth could put up with them provided they kept silent. Wired for sound, they went too far.

He gave Bill one long, reproachful look such as St Sebastian might have given his persecutors, and left the room in a marked manner.

To Bill it was as if he had been one of a

beleaguered garrison and the United States Marines, having arrived, had simply turned on their heels and gone off again. For some moments he continued standing where he was, his nose pressed against the pane; then reluctantly he grasped the water pipe and started to lower himself. He was oppressed by a bitter feeling that this was the last time he would put his faith in tall, thin chaps. 'Let me have men about me that are fat,' thought Bill, as he worked his way cautiously downwards.

The water pipe was magnificent. It could easily, if it had had the distorted sense of humour of some water pipes, have come apart from the wall and let him shoot down like a falling star, but it stood as firm as a rock. It did not even wobble. And Bill's heart, which had been in his mouth, gradually returned to its base. Something resembling elation crept into his mood. He might have missed seeing Prudence, but he had outsmarted Lady Hermione Wedge, the man with the service revolver, the unseen Thomas, and the mysterious Charles. They had pitted their wits against his, and he must have made them feel uncommonly foolish.

This elation reached its peak as he felt the solid earth beneath his feet. But it did not maintain its new high for long. Almost immediately there was a sharp drop, and his heart, rocketing up once more, returned to his mouth. A rich smell of pig assailed his nostrils, and a thin, piping voice spoke behind him.

'Wah yah dah?' said the voice.

The speaker was a very small man in corduroy trousers, niffy to a degree and well stricken in years. He might have been either a smelly centenarian or an octogenarian who had been prematurely aged by trouble. A stranger to Bill, he would have been recognized immediately by Lady Hermione Wedge, to whom both his appearance and aroma were familiar. He was Lord Emsworth's pig man, Edwin Pott, and the reason he said 'Wah yah dah?' when he meant 'What are you doing?' was that he had no roof to his mouth. One does not blame him for this. As Gally had said to Lady Hermione, we can't all have roofs to our mouths. One simply mentions it.

The point is perhaps a moot one, but it is probably better, when you are caught sliding down water pipes outside other people's houses, if your captor is a man with a roof to his mouth and not one lacking this useful property. In the former case, some sort of exchange of ideas is possible, in the latter not. When Edwin Pott said 'Wah yah dah?' Bill could not follow him.

He made, accordingly, no reply, and the other, seeming to feel that the burden of the conversation was up to him, said: 'Car yar, har?' To this question, too, Bill made no response. He would have been, in any event, disinclined for talk. What he wanted to do was to remove himself as speedily as possible, and with this end in view he began to move round his companion like a large steamer circling a small buoy.

His progress was arrested. When Edwin Pott had said, 'Car yar, har?' he had meant 'Cotched you, have I?' and he now proceeded to suit action to words by clutching at Bill's coat and seizing it in a senile grasp. Bill endeavoured to release himself, but the hand held firm.

It was a situation with which Bill frankly did not know how to cope. We have spoken of him as a young man whose name would have come high up on the list of anyone looking for a deputy to tackle a mad bull for him, and with a mad bull he would have known where he was. Nor would he have been at a loss if Edwin Pott had been some powerful thug. With such antagonists he could have expressed himself.

But this was different. Here he was confronted by a poor human wreck with one foot in the grave and the other sliding towards it, a frail wisp of a creature whose white hairs, such of them as still lingered on his egg-shaped head, claimed chivalry and respect. He could have recommended Edwin Pott a good lung tonic. He could not haul off and sock him on the jaw.

Once more he tried chivalrously and respectfully to loosen the clutching hand. It was in vain. 'Come one, come all, this rock shall fly from its firm base as soon as I,' Edwin Pott seemed to be saying. The situation had arrived at what is commonly known as a deadlock. Bill wanted to get away but was unable to do so. Edwin Pott wanted to shout for assistance but could produce only a thin, shrill sound like the whistling of gas in a pipe. (His vocal cords had never been the same since the evening during the last General

Election when he had strained them while addressing the crowd at the public bar of the Emsworth Arms in the Conservative interest.)

It was on this picture in still life that Colonel Wedge now intruded with his service revolver.

In supposing that by climbing down the water pipe he had outsmarted Colonel Wedge Bill had been laughably in error. You might outsmart captains by such tactics, and perhaps majors, but not colonels. The possibility of the existence of such a pipe had flashed upon Egbert Wedge at the moment when Charles, enjoying himself for the first time, for every footman likes smashing his employer's property, had started to break down Prudence's door, and it had sent him racing for the stairs. You do not have to tell a military man anything about the importance of cutting off the enemy's retreat.

His first emotion on beholding the group before him was a stern joy mingled with cordial appreciation of his cleverness and foresight; his second a strong feeling of relief that he had got his service revolver with him. Seen at close range, this marauding blighter looked an unpleasantly tough marauding blighter, the very type of marauding blighter for whose undoing you need all the service revolvers you can get. He found himself marvelling that Edwin Pott had had the intrepidity to engage in hand-to-hand combat so extraordinarily well-nourished a specimen of the criminal classes, and immediately decided that he personally was not going to do anything so damn silly.

'Hands up, you feller!' he cried, opening the

271

proceedings at a comfortable distance. He had intended to say 'scoundrel', but the word had escaped him in the heat of the moment.

'Ar car har,' said Edwin Pott rather smugly, and Colonel Wedge, who was something of a linguist, correctly understanding him to have explained that it was he who had cotched the miscreant, gave credit where credit was due.

'Smart work, Pott,' he said. 'Right ho, Pott, stand aside. I'm going to march him up to the house.'

Although he had anticipated some such development, Bill could not restrain a cry.

'Silence!' barked Colonel Wedge in his parade voice. 'Right-about turn, quick march, and don't try any of your larks. This revolver's loaded.'

With an imperious gesture he motioned Bill to precede him, and Bill, feeling that any show of disinclination on his part would be classed by this severe critic under the head of trying larks, did so. Colonel Wedge followed, his weapon at the ready, and Edwin Pott, in his capacity of principal witness for the prosecution, brought up the rear. The procession moved round the corner of the house and approached the terrace.

The Hon. Galahad was standing on the terrace, apparently in a reverie. He looked up as they drew near, having become aware of Edwin Pott, from whose direction a light breeze was blowing. At the sight of Bill, the revolver, the colonel, and the pig man, a surprised expression came into his face. He had been wondering what had become of his young friend, but he had never expected that anything like this had happened to him.

'Good Lord, Bill,' he ejaculated, screwing his monocle more tightly into his eye. 'What's all this?'

Colonel Wedge was surprised in his turn. He had not known that burglars moved in such influential circles.

'Bill? Do you know this frightful chap?'

'Know him? Many a time I've dandled him on my knee.'

'You couldn't have done,' said Colonel Wedge, running his eye over Bill's substantial frame. 'There wouldn't have been room.'

'When he was a baby,' explained Gally.

'Oh, when he was a baby? You mean you knew him as a baby?'

'Intimately'

'What sort of baby was he?'

'Delightful.'

'Well, he's changed a lot since then,' said Colonel Wedge, breaking the bad news regretfully. 'He's become the most ghastly outsider. Burgles houses at six o'clock in the evening.'

'Ar car har,' said Edwin Pott.

'Pott cotched him,' translated the colonel. 'The chap was sliding down a water pipe.'

Bill felt it time to put in a word.

'I wanted to find Prue, Gally. I saw her standing on a balcony, and I went and fetched a ladder.'

'Quite right,' said Gally approvingly. 'Did you have a nice talk?'

'She wasn't there. But she had left a letter for me. It's all right, Gally. She still loves me.'

'So she gave me to understand when I was chatting with her. Well, that's fine.'

Enlightenment had come upon Colonel Wedge. 'Good God! Is this the chap Hermione was telling me about?'

'Yes, this is Prue's demon lover.'

'Well, I'm dashed. I took him for a burglar. I'm sorry.'

'Not at all,' said Bill.

'Afraid you must have thought me a bit abrupt just now.'

'No, no,' said Bill. 'Quite all right.'

Colonel Wedge found himself in something of a quandary. A romantic at heart, his wife's revelations of the tangled love affair of his niece Prudence had left him sensible of a sneaking sympathy for the young man of her choice. Unpleasant it must have been for the chap, he felt, to have his bride whisked away on the wedding morning and kept in storage under lock and key. Not the sort of thing he would have liked himself. He was also an admirer of spirit in the young of the male sex, and Bill's thrustful policy in the matter of ladders and water pipes appealed to him.

On the other hand, he was a loyal husband and he knew that his wife felt very strongly on the subject of the fellow. Not once but many times she had spoken of him in terms which left no room for misunderstanding.

'Do you know, Gally,' he said, 'I think I'll be popping off. I don't want to be mixed up with this. See what I mean?'

The Hon. Galahad saw what he meant and

thought his policy prudent.

'Yes, no need for you to stick around, Egbert. Buzz off. And,' he added, indicating Edwin Pott, who had withdrawn respectfully into the background until his offices as a witness should be required, 'take that odoriferous gargoyle with you. I've something to say to Bill in private.'

Colonel Wedge strode off, followed by Edwin Pott, and a grave look came into Gally's face.

'Bill,' he began, 'I'm sorry to tell you that a rather unfortunate thing has happened. Oh, blast it,' he broke off, for he saw that they were about to be interrupted.

Tipton Plimsoll had appeared on the terrace.

'There's someone coming,' he said, jerking an explanatory thumb.

Bill looked round. And as he saw the tall, thin chap who had so signally fallen short at their last meeting in hospitality and indeed in the first principles of humanity, his face darkened. His was as a rule a mild and equable nature, but Tipton's behaviour on that occasion had aroused his indignation. He wanted a word with him.

'Hi!' he said, advancing.

There had crept into Tipton Plimsoll's face a sudden expression of grim determination. It was the sort of look you might have seen on the faces of the Light Brigade when the order came to charge. He had not thought of it before, but it came to him now that there was a special technique which knowledgeable people employed with phantoms. They walked through them. He had read stories where fellows had done this, and always with the happiest results.

The phantoms, realizing that they had run up against something hot, faltered, lost their nerve, and withdrew from the unequal contest.

If there had been any other avenue to a peaceful settlement, he would have taken it, for it was a thing he was not at all anxious to do. But there seemed no alternative. You have got to be firm with phantoms.

Commending his soul to God, he lowered his head and drove forward at Bill's midriff.

'Oof!' said Bill.

'Cheese!' said Tipton.

It would not be easy to say which of the two was the more astonished, or which the more filled with honest indignation. But Bill being occupied with the task of recovering his breath, Tipton was the first to give expression to his feelings.

'Well, how was I to know he was real?' he demanded, turning to Gally as a fair-minded non-partisan who would be able to view the situation objectively. 'This guy's been following me around for days, dodging in and out of registry offices, popping around corners, leering at me out of shrubberies. And it isn't more than about half a minute ago that he was snooping in at my window. If he thinks I'm going to stand for that sort of thing, he's darned well mistaken. There's a limit,' said Tipton, summing up.

Once more the congenial task of pouring oil on troubled waters had fallen to the Hon. Galahad. Tipton's revelations in his bedroom on the previous day had placed him in the position of being able to understand that which he might otherwise have found a perplexing state of affairs.

'You don't mean to tell me it's Bill you've been seeing all this time? How very remarkable. This is my godson, Bill Lister. Tipton Plimsoll, Bill, nephew of my old friend Chet Tipton. When did you two first meet? At Barribault's Hotel, was it not?'

'He came rubbering through the glass door when I was in the bar.'

'Well, I wanted a drink,' said Bill defensively. 'I was being married that morning.'

'Married?' Tipton was beginning to understand all and to be in a position to forgive all. 'Was that why you were at that registry office?'

'Yes.'

'Well, I'm darned.'

'The whole matter,' said Gally, 'is susceptible of a ready explanation. His bride, my niece Prudence, was arrested by the authorities before she could get to the registry office and sent down here. Bill followed. That was how you happened to meet.'

Tipton's whole manner had softened. He had even begun to smile. But now the recollection of a particular grievance hardened him again.

'There was no need for him to wear that gosh-awful beard,' he said.

'There was every need,' said Gally. 'He had to avoid recognition. And when he made faces outside your window, I imagine he was just coming from my niece's room, which adjoins yours. Am I right, Bill?'

'Yes. I was walking along a sort of ledge and I

saw him in his room and I wanted him to let me in. But he just stared at me and went out.'

'And now, of course, you appreciate his motives in doing so. I remember a dear old friend of mine, Boko Bagshott — dead now, I'm sorry to say. Cirrhosis of the liver — who frequently saw faces at windows, and he was always off like a scalded cat the moment they appeared. In fairness I don't think we can blame Plimsoll.'

'I suppose not,' said Bill, though grudgingly.

'One must always try to put oneself in the other fellow's place. You could hardly have expected him in the circumstances to extend a warm southern welcome.'

'I suppose not,' said Bill, less grudgingly.

As far as Tipton Plimsoll was concerned, the whole unpleasant matter was now forgotten. The smile which had stolen into his face and receded returned with increased brilliance. It became a grin which would have made an excellent substitute for the evening sunlight, if the latter had for any reason decided to cease to illuminate the terrace.

'Gosh,' he said, 'this is a weight off my mind. This is where I begin to live. You don't know what it's been like this last week, never being able to take the slightest snifter without seeing a hideous — without seeing a face bob up in the offing. I couldn't have stuck it out much longer. Mind you, now that I'm going to be married — '

'Are you going to be married?'

'You betcher.'

'Congratulations,' said Bill.

278

'Thanks, old man,' said Tipton.

'I hope you will be very, very happy, old man,' said Bill.

'I'll do just that little thing, old man,' said Tipton. 'As I was saying,' he went on, resuming his remarks, 'now that I'm going to be married, I've finished with all the rough stuff and I don't suppose I shall go on another real toot for the rest of my life, except of course on New Year's Eve — '

'Of course,' said Bill.

' — and Boat Race Night — '

'Naturally,' said Bill.

' — and special occasions like that,' said Tipton. 'But it's nice to know that one will be able to lower the stuff in strict moderation. It makes you feel so darned silly, swigging barley water when the rest of the boys are having highballs. Yes, it's certainly been a life-saver, running into you.'

' 'Running into' is right,' said Bill.

'Ha, ha,' said Tipton, laughing heartily.

'Ha, ha,' said Bill, also laughing heartily.

Tipton slapped Bill's back. Bill slapped Tipton's. The Hon. Galahad beamed with growing approval on this delightful scene of cordiality and good feeling. He now asked Tipton if he would be offended if he were to take his godson to one side and impart to him something which was exclusively for his personal ear; and Tipton said: 'Go ahead, go right ahead.' Gally said they would be only half a minute, and Tipton said: 'Take your time, take your time, take your time.'

'Bill,' said Gally, leading him to the terrace wall and speaking in a low, urgent voice, 'we have come to a crisis in your affairs. It's most unfortunate that you should have formed such a warm friendship with this chap Plimsoll.'

'He seems a good sort.'

'A capital young fellow. Grouchy when I first met him, but now the living image of his uncle Chet, who was the most carefree soul who ever wrecked a restaurant. Very rich.'

'Is he?'

'Enormously. And I feel he likes you.'

'I thought he was matey.'

'Yes, I think you have made an excellent first impression. And everything now depends on him.'

'How do you mean?'

A rather sombre look had come into the Hon. Galahad's monocle.

'I was telling you, when he came up, that an unfortunate thing had happened. Prue's original plan, if you remember, was to get the capital for modernizing and running the Mulberry Tree from my brother Clarence. And with that necklace under our belts this could have been done. Prue told you about the necklace in her letter?'

'Yes. It struck me as the goods.'

'It was the goods. With it in our possession, we should have been able to dictate terms. Most unfortunately, I've lost it.'

'What!'

'It has been pinched. I went to my room just now, to make sure it was there, and it wasn't.'

'Oh, my aunt!'

Gally shook his head.

'It isn't your aunt that matters, it's Prue's. There is just a chance that it isn't Hermione who has got the thing, but if she has, our flank is turned and only one hope remains. We must try to get that capital from young Plimsoll.'

'But I can't. We've only just met.'

'Quite. But his feelings towards you are obviously warm. I got the impression that he was so much obliged to you for not being a spectre that you would be able to ask of him anything you wished, even unto half his kingdom. At any rate, his are the ribs we must endeavour to get into. Tails up, and leave the talking to me. Dash it,' said Gally, with much the same gallant spirit as had animated Freddie when about to broach the subject of Donaldson's Dog-Joy to Major R. B. and Lady Emily Finch, 'I've talked the hind legs off the toughest bookies in my time and defeated in debate bouncers at all the principal bars both in London and New York. I should not fail now.'

VI

'Tell me, my dear Plimsoll,' said Gally. 'Or may I call you Tipton?'

'Why, sure,' said Tipton. 'Or, rather, Tippy. You, too,' he added handsomely.

'Thanks, Tippy,' said Bill.

'Not at all,' said Tipton. 'Delighted.'

The Hon. Galahad allowed his monocle to

play upon him like a sunbeam, well pleased that such a delightful atmosphere of camaraderie should have been established at the very outset of the negotiations.

'What I was about to ask you, my dear Tippy,' he said, 'was, have you ever given a thought to modern trends?'

'Well, I'll tell you,' said Tipton, learning for the first time that these existed, 'what with one thing and another, no.'

'When I say 'modern trends',' proceeded Gally, 'I am thinking at the moment of the amusement world. Amazing how people's tastes have altered since I was your age. *Tempora mutantur, nos et mutumur in illis.*'

'You betcher,' said Tipton, fogged but courteous.

'Take the simple matter of having a drink. In my young days one just went down the street to a bar.'

'And not at all a bad thing to do,' said Tipton.

'Quite. But see how the motor-car has changed all that. The cry now is all for the great outdoors. The fellow with a thirst grabs the nearest girl, dumps her in his automobile, and ho for the open spaces. Instead of suffocating in some smelly bar in London they take their refreshment on the cool terrace swept by the healthy breezes of a country inn outside Oxford.'

'Oxford?'

'Oxford.'

'Why Oxford particularly?' asked Tipton.

'Because,' said Gally, 'that is the modern trend. Oxford is a nice easy distance, and you are right away from all the stuffiness of London. A man who owns an inn anywhere near Oxford is a man to be envied.'

'I guess so,' said Tipton.

'Such a man, to take an instance, as Bill.'

'Bill?'

'Bill.'

'This Bill?'

'That's the one,' said Gally. 'He is the proprietor of a picturesque inn not far from Oxford, and what I have been telling him is that if he branches out and turns the place into what they call in your country a roadhouse with all the modern improvements, he has a gold mine. You probably agree with me?'

'Oh, sure.'

'I thought you would. Properly developed, this inn of Bill's would be a bonanza.'

'I'll say.'

'It is situated in the most delightful spot of one of England's most delightful counties. People would come from miles around merely to look at the scenery. Add a first-class cellar, squash racket courts, a jazz band and really fine cooking, perfectly served — out of doors on the terrace in good weather, in the richly panelled dining-room when it was wet — and you would have something which would draw the automobile trade like a magnet.'

'Is the dining-room richly panelled?'

'Not yet. I was going to touch on that point. To develop this place — the Mulberry Tree is its name — will require capital.'

'Sure. You can't branch out without capital.'

'I close my eyes,' said Gally, doing so, 'and I seem to see the Mulberry Tree as it will be when all the improvements are completed. Turning in off the main road, we drive through a fairylike garden studded with coloured lanterns.'

'With a fountain in the middle.'

'With, of course, a fountain in the middle.'

'Lit up with coloured lights.'

'Lit up, as you say, with coloured lights. I really am delighted at the way you are taking hold, my dear Tippy. I knew that I should interest you.'

'Oh, you do. Where were we?'

'We had reached the fountain. To our right are wide, spreading gardens, rich in every variety of flower; to our left, through the dim, mysterious trees, we catch a glimpse of shimmering silver.'

'Do we?' said Tipton. 'Why's that?'

'The swimming pool,' explained Gally.

'There's a swimming pool, is there?'

'There will be — once we have got the capital.'

Tipton reflected.

'I'd have artificial waves.'

'An admirable idea.'

'Artificial waves make such a difference.'

'All the difference. Make a note of artificial waves, Bill.'

'Right ho, Gally.'

'We then approach the terrace.'

'That's where the dinner is?'

'If the night is fine.'

'Look,' said Tipton, beginning to take fire, 'I'll tell you about that terrace. Make it a bower of roses.'

'We will.'

'You want one of those things you have over things. What *are* those things you have over things?'

'Umbrellas?' hazarded Bill.

'Bill!' said Gally reproachfully. 'You can't get an umbrella to smell like roses. You know that. The word Tippy is searching for, I imagine, is 'pergolas'.'

'Pergolas. That's right. You've got to have a rose-covered pergola, and you hide your jazz band behind a mass of luxurious honeysuckle. Gosh, it'll be great,' said Tipton, snapping his fingers. 'How much per head for dinner?'

'Eight shillings, I thought.'

'Make it ten bob. No one will ever know the difference. Well, look. Call it on an average night two hundred dinners at ten bob a nob, that's a hundred quid right out of the box. And when you reflect that that's going on all through the summer . . . And then there are the drinks. Don't forget the drinks. That's where the big profit comes in. Cocktails would be served on little tables around the fountain.'

'And on the brink of the swimming pool.'

Tipton had begun to pace up and down, expressing his emotion in sweeping gestures.

'Bill,' he said, 'you're on to a big thing.'

'I think so, Tippy.'

'Yessir, big. Folks'll come from all over the country. You won't be able to keep them away with an injunction. They'll have to tell off a special squad of cops to handle the traffic. You'll be a millionaire before you know where you are.'

'That's what I tell him,' said Gally. 'Really, one

sees no limits to the enterprise.'

'None,' agreed Tipton.

'There only remains this trifling matter of the capital.'

'The capital. Sure.'

'Get the capital, and we can start to-morrow.'

'Get the capital, and you're home.'

'Three thousand might do it.'

'Four would be safer.'

'Or five.'

'Yes, maybe five. Yes, five's the figure I see.'

Gally laid an affectionate hand on Tipton's shoulder and massaged it.

'You would really be prepared to put up five thousand pounds?' he asked tenderly.

Tipton stared.

'Me? Put up five thousand pounds? I'm not going to put up anything,' he said, chuckling a little at the bizarreness of the idea. 'Why, I might lose my money. But I guess you'll get your capital all right. Ask around. And now you'll have to excuse me. I promised to take Vee for a row on the lake.'

He gambolled off, the picture of youth and life and happiness. It is possible that he may have known that he was leaving aching hearts behind him, but not probable. Tipton Plimsoll was a rather self-centred young man.

VII

Gally looked at Bill. Bill looked at Gally. For a moment neither spoke, their thoughts being too deep for words. Then Gally made an observation which he had once heard from the lips of a disappointed punter at a suburban race meeting on the occasion of his finding that the bookmaker with whom he had wagered on the winner of the last race had packed up and disappeared, leaving no address. It seemed to relieve him. His manner became calmer.

'Well, that's that, Bill.'

'That's that, Gally.'

'An extraordinarily similar thing happened to an old friend of mine many years ago, when he was trying to interest a wealthy young man in a club which he was planning to open. He told me with tears in his eyes, I remember, that he could have betted his entire fortune, if he had had one, that the chap was just about to reach for his cheque book. These things do happen. One must accept them with grim fortitude. We now come back to Clarence. I'd give anything to know if Hermione has got that necklace. If she hasn't, it may be possible to achieve the happy ending by means of a little inspired bluffing. Ah, here she comes.'

Bill leaped like a hooked worm.

'Eh? What? Where?' He cast a feverish eye towards the house and saw that the bad news was only too true. Lady Hermione, accompanied by Lord Emsworth, had just come through the French windows of the drawing-room. 'Gally, I'm off'.

The Hon. Galahad nodded.

'Yes, I think perhaps it would be best if you left me to handle the negotiations. If I were you,

I'd go and have a chat with Prue. I saw her just now going in the direction of the rose garden. You will find the rose garden over there,' said Gally, pointing. 'I'll join you later,' he said, and turned to meet his flesh and blood, who were now making their way towards him across the terrace. His face was hard and determined. His monocle gleamed with quiet resolution. He looked like a featherweight contender entering the ring to do battle with the champion.

It was as his sister drew near and he was able to study her face that a sudden quick hope strengthened his doughty heart. Hers, it seemed to him, was not the air of a woman who by getting her hooks on necklaces has outgeneralled the opposition. It was unmistakably one of gloom.

'Tails up!' said Gally to his heart, and his heart replied, 'You betcher.'

In supposing Lady Hermione to be gloomy, Gally had been right. It is fortunately only very rarely that in any given family in the English upper classes you will find two members of it who have drained the bitter cup in a single afternoon. The average of mental anguish is as a rule lower. But this had happened to-day. We have shown Colonel Wedge frankly confessing that he had done so, and Lady Hermione, if questioned, would have been obliged to make the same admission. As she came on to the terrace, her spirits were at a very low ebb and she was recognizing the outlook as unsettled.

To the best of her knowledge, the necklace still remained in her brother Galahad's possession, and his prediction that she would be compelled to throw in the towel still rang in her ears. The more she contemplated the position of affairs, the more sadly convinced did she become that he was right, and a proud woman dislikes having to throw in towels. But she could see no way out of it.

Freddie, delivering his ultimatum at the general meeting, had seemed to her to speak with the voice of doom. Were he to carry out his threat of telling all to Tipton Plimsoll, disaster must ensue. She had been deeply impressed by the haughty and imperious spirit which Tipton had shown when switching necklaces from spot to spot in the drawing-room. There, she had felt, stood a man who would stand no nonsense. Let him discover that he had been deceived, and he would break off the engagement. And at the thought of her child losing such a mate, she quailed.

It would be but a poor consolation to her in later years, when people were congragulating her on Veronica's marriage to the reasonably eligible husband whom the future would no doubt produce, to tell them that they ought to have seen the one that got away.

Reflections such as these had weakened her once iron will. She was beginning to think that there were more important things in life than checking the impulse of her sister Dora's daughter to marry into the Underworld. She had not revised her opinion that Bill was the dregs of humanity, but there had began to steal over her the feeling that it was Dora's place, not hers, to do the worrying.

She was, in short, but a shell of her former self. She had become a defeatist.

Gally was a man who believed in brisk attack. He wasted no time in preliminaries.

'Well?' he said.

Lady Hermione quivered, but was silent.

'Made up your mind?' said Gally.

There was almost a pleading note in Lady Hermione's voice as she endeavoured to reason with him.

'But, Galahad, you can't want your niece to marry a penniless artist?'

'He isn't a penniless artist. He's the owner of what will be the finest roadhouse in England as soon as Clarence has put up the capital for modernization and improvements.'

'Eh?' said Lord Emsworth, whose thoughts had wandered.

'Listen, Clarence,' said Gally. 'Do you want to make a lot of money?'

'I've got a lot of money,' said Lord Emsworth.

'You can always do with a bit more.'

'True.'

'Picture to yourself, Clarence,' said Gally, 'a fair countryside, and in that countryside a smiling inn. Its grounds,' he hurried on, for he could see that his brother was about to ask why the inn was smiling, 'are dotted — very profusely dotted — with groups sucking down cocktails at a couple of bob a go. Its terrace is a solid mass of diners enjoying the ten-shilling dinner under a bower of roses. There are lanterns. There is a fountain, lit by coloured lights. There is a

290

swimming pool with — mark this, Clarence — artificial waves. It is, in short, the most popular place of its kind in the country, the turnover being terrific.'

Lord Emsworth said it sounded nice, and Gally assured him that he had found the *mot juste*.

'A gold mine,' he said. 'And a half share in it, Clarence, is yours for five thousand pounds.'

'Five thousand pounds?'

'You can hardly believe it, can you? A mere pittance. And no need,' said Gally, seeing that the other had become meditative, 'to dig up the money on the nail. All I want from you is a letter to my godson, Bill Lister, promising to cough up in due course.'

Lord Emsworth had begun to fiddle with his pince-nez — a bad sign, in Gally's opinion. He had often seen bank managers fiddle with their pince-nez when he looked in to arrange about an overdraft.

'Well, I don't know, Galahad.'

'Come, come, Clarence.'

'Five thousand pounds is a great deal of money.'

'A sprat to catch a whale. You'll see it back at the end of the first year. Did I mention that there would be a first-class jazz orchestra playing behind a mass of honeysuckle?'

Lord Emsworth shook his head.

'I'm sorry, Galahad — '

Gally's face hardened.

'All right,' he said. 'Then mark the alternative. I stick to that necklace, and what ensues? Ruin and misery and desolation. Young Plimsoll breaks off his engagement to Veronica. Mrs Freddie divorces Freddie.'

'Eh?'

'And poor old Freddie, I suppose, comes to eke out the sad remainder of his days at Blandings Castle.'

'What!'

'It seems the logical thing for him to do. The wounded bird creeping back to the old nest. You'll like having Freddie at Blandings. Nice company for your declining years.'

Lord Emsworth recovered the pince-nez which had leaped from his nose. On his face, as he replaced them, there was the look of one who has come to a decision.

'I'll go and write that letter at once,' he said. 'The name is Lister?'

'William Lister,' said Gally. 'L for Laryngitis, I for Ipecacuanha, S for — '

But Lord Emsworth had gone.

'Ha!' said Gally, removing his hat and fanning with it a brow which had become a little heated.

His sister Hermione, too, seemed to be under a sense of strain. Her eyes were bulging, and there was a tinge of purple in her cheeks.

'And now, perhaps, Galahad,' she said, 'you will be good enough to give me that necklace.'

There was a brief pause. It was as if the Hon. Galahad shrank from saying what he feared might wound.

'I haven't got it.'

'What!'

'I'm sorry. Not my fault. I'll tell you exactly

292

what happened,' said Gally, with manly regret. 'From motives of safety, in case you might feel the urge to come and hunt about in my room, I put it in a place where I thought you wouldn't dream of looking. Yesterday young Plimsoll gave me his flask to keep for him — a large, roomy flask — '

He paused. A stricken cry had rung through the quiet garden. Lady Hermione was looking like a cook who has seen a black beetle in her kitchen and the last of the beetle powder used up yesterday.

'You put the necklace in Tipton's flask?'

'A dashed shrewd hiding place, I thought. But I'm sorry to say the bally thing has been removed. Who has got it now I can't tell you.'

'I can,' said Lady Hermione. 'He gave it to me. I met him coming out of my room just now, and he pressed it into my hand with a strange, wild look in his eyes, and asked me to take care of it for him.'

Her voice trailed away in a sigh that was like the wind blowing through the cracks in a broken heart.

'Galahad,' she said, 'you ought to have been a confidence man.'

'So people have told me,' said Gally, flattered. 'Well, that's fine. If you've got the thing, you can give it to Freddie, and the matter is closed. Everybody happy, loving young hearts united, nothing to worry about. And now I'll go and see how Clarence is getting on with that letter. After that, I have to go and meet a couple of people in the rose garden.'

He trotted off towards the house, going hippety-hippety-hop like an elderly Christopher Robin.